RJ STEPHENS

D1745186

1

MOON

XHOSETI

Books also by this author:

XHOSETI — FIRST CONTACT

XHOSETI — AD 2492

MOON

ROBERT J

STEPHENS

XHOSETI

MOON

XHOSETJ

4

MOON

For my father, who sowed the seeds for this book a long... long time ago!

MOON

"Mortem est ad vitam procreandi!"

"Death is necessary for life to procreate!"

RJ Stephens, 2018

SOLAR

SYSTEM

EARTH

MOON

Chapter One

24 Million miles from Earth

Without an environment to transfer sound silence was all that could be heard in space. No carbon-based life form could survive its freezing grasp. Nothing and no living entity could withstand the grasp of its freezing maul.

Nothing moved; nothing stirred, nothing loved, nothing fought, nothing gave or took life...Space is just that...Space. Nothing interacted with nothing.

Space is...

COLD... DARK... STERILE.

But zoom in just a little on a particular part of the solar system and that *nothing* is active, *very active.* Small boulders each the size of a house clash and collide forming alliances as clans did back on Earth many thousands of years ago. The violent merger was simply a product born from the need to survive. Sometimes profit or simply greed would initiate the bonding of the Earth-bound families. Eventually, the time driven melding formed a bigger, stronger, more dominant house that would rise above the corpse of the now desiccated forgotten remains of the old discarded house. A useful but now defunct stepping stone on the path towards immortality. Others drift silently and slowly towards each other, enticed by the dance of a joining to become one entity, melded together in the embrace of gravity. The act of merging was as if two lovers were courting each other both striving towards the same goal and when the final embrace materialised something new, bigger and better was born.

Gravity was predictable. Governed by the laws of physics, each asteroid's movements could be tracked, calculated, plotted and even their merging dances predicted.

Look even closer and all was not what it appeared to be. A small cluster of boulders on the very outskirt of the asteroid belt appeared to make sudden flitting movements when approached by any debris. These movements allowed the offending embrace seeking piece of inert rock to pass through their ranks unhindered. Hundreds of randomly appearing car sized boulders moved and flirted with each other all with a seeming effortless fluidity.

If one were to fly directly above these randomly scattered, seemingly intelligent rocks, a pattern, barely discernable started to emerge. At the very tip of the now discernable spearhead, a slightly larger boulder appears to pulse and radiate with a soft reddish glow. The glow,

9

barely discernible above the oxide covered boulders of the other rocks in the nearby asteroid belt, pulsed with a timely frequency. Two columns of smaller boulders stretched southwards from it. If the tip of the spearhead lay north, the southward running columns appeared to be separated from each other by an all-inclusive angle of seventy degrees. At the very southern side of the spear head, splitting the centreline of the two columns, lay another slightly larger boulder, this one pulsing with a slightly bluish tinge. It too was at the apex of a spearhead although an inverted one. The columns of the blue faction run northwards towards the larger red pulsing boulder, they too are separated by an angle of thirty-seven and a half degrees to the projected centre line of the loosely formed structure. Where the two spear-like columns intersect is what appears to be a large diamond shaped void. Nothing appears to enter or leave that volume of space. It is as if one was gazing directly into the mouth of a huge dark forbidding cavern, the vacuum of the nothingness projecting power and menace. Looking into its darkness one began to feel drawn in...no...sucked in by the magnetism of the gravitational pull exerted by its shear lack of presence.

All is quiet...All is peaceful...All is in balance...

*

MOON

EARTH

MOON

MOON

Chapter Two

AD 2750

Moon

Luke was doing his rounds again...for the third time. Employed as a security guard for the Galactic Mining Corporation. He loved that name,

*"Galactic my foot! Huh!...*In name only, they still need foot plodders like me though!" The corporation mined the *Moon* and the *Earth*, what was so *Galactic* about that he mused?

"Careful Luke, we can hear everything you say, that last comment will not look good in your file. You know that everything you say is transcribed directly to disk and then sealed," said the voice through his helmet speaker.

These late-night shifts had their benefits though; no one to bust his balls, especially that bitch of a hag, his boss Lynette. He was sure she had made her way through the ranks purely based on blackmail. She must have something really graphic on the director to have landed this cushy number. Still could be worse, he could be sitting next to her for his full shift! This way he got to go down into the guts of the machine that hummed and whirred; all that gigantic machinery just to generate some

12

kind of kinetic energy that was beamed down to the defence ring that surrounded the *Earth.*

Built back in the early twenty fourth century, the ring not only served as a defence platform to defend the Earth against any *Xhoseti* invasion; but had also been used to clean the atmosphere ridding it of the last remnants of the fallout dust cloud.

The last war had been a nuclear one and the dust clouds that had been thrown into the stratosphere had blocked out the sun's nourishing rays. Once the atmosphere had been cleaned, the planet had been on the road to full recovery. Man could start repopulating the Earth. The animals and plants had been allowed back into the recovering grasslands and woodlands. Things were almost pre-twentieth century. The only blip on the horizon was mankind's constant need for energy.

This time though, under instruction of the *Guardians,* there was to be no fossil fuels used in the generation of electricity. Wind turbines provided a small amount of electricity for power grids once the *Domes* the *ATS* machines were powering came down.

Were they machines?

13

MOON

It was difficult to explain what they were; what kind of machine could change its shape like that? Something was very strange about them! It was almost as if they were watching us, as the *Guardians* had watched and guided man's rise towards civilisation and eventually its demise over the past forty or so thousand years.

Then there was the alignment of the planets and the firing of the pyramid weapons back in AD 2492. Every kid knew the story. It was drummed into them during the start of every study year. Like their teaching methods or not, repetition eventually got through to even the thickest of human brains.

Shining his torch on one of the huge rotating balls of electricity generating turbines, he had an involuntary shudder, not one of revulsion though, but one of pure pleasure; seeing this great machine in operation always filled him with a sense of achievement. Not that he had anything to do with its design or construction, but merely the fact that man could achieve such a great thing on another ball of rock other than the Earth.

The additional gravity created by the spinning generators allowed him to walk along the handrail protected plastic grated walkway.

One of the most valuable commodities up on the *Moon* was water. That simple hydrogen and oxygen liquid that is in such abundance back down on Earth. Not only was it used for hydration and the daily sanitation rituals that the corporation insisted each member of its staff follow, it was also used to provide the breathable atmosphere in his suit. Each time he went out on patrol, he made sure that the vial in his suit was full of fresh, untarnished distilled water. The suit had kinetic electrical trickle chargers that slowly broke down the water to its base components and hence topped up his supply of breathable oxygen; the scrubbers dealt with the rest. Yet again he had another involuntary shudder, this time one of revulsion.

He recalled the first time he had seen them high up in the apex of the generator halls dome like structure. Rats, not just any type of rat though, huge mutated rats; how they had made their way up here was a mystery to him. The furry rodents had shed all their fur and been left a bright white colour as the Moon dust had coated their once pink bodies. *Moon* dust - now that really was a problem. The fine powdery like substance got into everything. Eventually shearing through any man-made substance. It acted like a cutting paste and with time and any fretting motion simply sawed its way through anything it rested on. The rats had terrible sores and scars all over

15

their bodies making them appear as if they had been spawned from very depths of hell.

Somehow these now de-furred rodents had managed to survive on the escaping gas and liquid every time someone opened or closed an airlock, though what they ate he could only imagine.

Then there was that red glowing fungus that seemed to cover the ceiling of the generator hall...looked like rust to him. He shone his high beam torch up towards the corner of one of the structural beams holding the ceiling in place and could just make out a denser patch of the fungus. It seemed to thrive on the energy of his torch beam and visibly extended itself towards the light; his torch started to flicker and waiver. He gave another involuntary shudder and shut the torch off, shaking it about until the kinetic motion recharged the torch's battery.

Walking in between the magnetically created fields of the generators, he could feel the tug and draw of each generator on his feet as he lifted first the left foot and then the right foot and tried to walk in a straight line. It was like some kind of quest for him to march as straight as possible along the grated walkway. Get it wrong and he could feel the tug of one generators magnetically created gravitational pull over the other. It felt as if his legs were being pulled apart by some gigantic unseen force intent on ripping him in two.

Urban legend had it that one of the apprentices leaned over the handrail intent on getting a better look at the rotating generator, some sort of clever engineering type, and was sucked into the field. The mess was never cleared up as the generators could not be stopped merely to scrape up the flattened remains of one hardly missed apprentice.

Maybe that's how the rats survived? Feeding of his remains, but how did the gravity not affect them?

"Nah, they must eat something else," Luke blurted out to himself forgetting yet again about the recording device.

Walking cautiously along the row of generators, he kept on glancing upwards as a frightened deer would when it could smell the scent of a predator, not knowing where it was, but knowing that it was there just waiting for the right moment to pounce.

It was then out of the corner of his eye he caught a slight movement up on the ceiling. There appeared to be a panicked flurry of movement and a tiny squeak and a hiss as one of the rats was dispatched by something unknown. He raised his torch and set it to high beam.

17

Something of an insectoid like shape scurried out of the light projected by the high beam, but not before he caught a glimpse of its red glowing eyes.

"Holy Shit, what the fuck was that?" he blurted out into his microphone.

"Come again Luke?" came the reply from control.

"This is control, please repeat – over," repeated Lynette.

"Luke, your heart rate and breathing have increased dramatically. Please calm down; take a few deep breaths. Breathe slowly and clearly. You are burning up your oxygen supply at an alarming rate, *calm yourself!* Remember the safety induction, count to ten, slowly; repeat if necessary. Breath in slowly, exhale slowly," came the instruction from control.

"Right...right, sorry, just got a bit of a scare, saw something take out one of the rats, something I haven't seen before."

"Well stop screwing around and get your ass back to the control centre, we have a briefing from the boss in twenty minutes – control out."

Luke waited a few seconds to regain his composure,

18

"Copy that, on my way."

*

Chris surveyed the extent of what was now the fastest expanding city on Earth–City Number One, Guardian. So named in honour of those *Moa* like suited *Guardians* who had presided over the rise of mankind's first civilization. Which also culminated in its final destruction and subsequent rebuilding.

Well that's public relations for you; destroy a planet and its inhabitants then rebuild it as you see fit and history will write you down as heroes. So little did the human population know of the past failures that he had been called upon to remedy.

Then there was the ultimate instruction given by the *Guardians* to initiate the start of World War Three. That information was only given to the selected few, his very own miniature paramilitary force. They were also sworn to secrecy upon their eighteenth-degree initiation. It was then and only then once they had sworn their fealty to him were they impregnated with their *Morph-Suits.* The grafting procedure was not as painful as he remembered his father describing to him and thankfully he had never had to undergo the process himself having received it while in the belly of the *ATS.*

19

MOON

There must be well in excess of a thousand converts by now. The *Guardians* had warned him that having an established covert secret police force would only breed suspicion and mistrust amongst the local population. Luckily, they went for the most part undetected, the general populous content to get on with their lives, making, trading, farming etc...etc. The details were not important.

Chris was just grateful that there had been no need to re-grow the *Green Giants* and use them as enforcers of the peace as they once had done during the Dome riots back in the early part of the fall-out period. Soon though, he predicted it would be time to re-grow the *Grey Engineers.* With the constant expansion rate of the cities more power constantly had to be sourced. The wind farms had been a good start, then came the hydro-electric schemes, after that the wave driven turbines; now there was the *Moon Grid,* an ingenious low gravity, almost frictionless, electricity generation dynamo plant.

The *ATS's* were instrumental in transporting the required materials, men and other resources required to build it. Volunteers had to be turned away, there were so many willing bodies trying to get onto the project. The created energy was transported via superconductors, naturally at near absolute zero degrees, to a firing station aimed at the defence ring. It was then beamed to a transforming station on the defence ring and modulated to be compatible with the receiving station down on Earth. The fly in the ointment so to speak was this confounded Moon dust! Every six months there was the inevitable severing of a component. The last one sheared a coupling on one of the main superconductors, putting the whole system out of commission for a week. Now redundancy systems had been put in place it was just a matter of constant maintenance, replacing components every six months to avoid the catastrophic outages that would inevitably happen without the part replacement program.

"Well that system needs to be changed, an upgrade is required," said *Chris* the now *Grand Master,* out loud.

The latest idea was to use the resources lying on the surface of the Moon and combine the depleted Helium 3 with Ununpentium MC115 first discovered in the early twenty first century but never found its way onto the list of viable energy sources, this lack of exploitation came down purely to shortfall of resources, both human and financial.

With a magnetic containment field similar to that currently in use on the existing generators, there should be very few issues with regards to generating enough gravitational spin to meld the two components together.

21

The resulting ball of energy would then be sent to the defence ring complete with its own containment housing and used as a source of energy which could then be catapulted down to the existing receiving stations. A few minor modifications would need to be enacted but that was all well within his engineer's capabilities.

First though, he had to supervise the down loading of the *Guardians* from their *Moa* life support suits to a more robust life support system. This was under direct request of his grandfather who was acknowledged to be the leader of the *Guardians*.

Chris wondered where his *ATS* could have got to. For the past six months he had not seen or heard from the bio-mechanical entity, which was very strange, having been a part of his daily life and life sustaining support system for over twenty-seven hundred years. He acknowledged that he did not own the *ATS*. It was not his pet to do his bidding when and how he felt. Then there was that tingling feeling on the back of his neck every time the *ATS* was near; he had even begun to feel a slight resentment emanating from the normally benign *ATS* every time he entered it to regenerate. Something had changed in his relationship with the *ATS*; maybe it just needed some time on its own.

Where did it get its power from?

22

The *ATS* always seemed to be full of energy, life even. He had seen it regenerate using seawater after barely surviving the attack from the pyramid weapon back in Egypt, but that surely could not be the source of its seemingly limitless power. No...There must be something else that powered his *ATS* and for that matter the *Guardian's* ones as well.

Over the past many hundreds of years he had started to get a feel for the *ATS's* personality, benign but with an agenda. What that agenda was *Chris* still needed to find out, but he was sure it was something on a massive scale, too big for even him to comprehend. But lately it had seemed as if the *ATS* was sulking and every time he needed to travel somewhere it always took longer than he remembered it taking in the past. It was as if the *ATS* was running out of power,

"Maybe it has just gone to recharge?"

*

MOON

XHOSETI

MOON

RJ STEPHENS

EARTH

MOON

Chapter Three

Earth

Arctic Circle

Chris entered the space jumper slightly bemused that he had to use this primitive form of transport to go to oversee the *Guardian* venting procedure. According to his grandfather, the *Patterns of Chaos* oracle machine found on *Termite* had predicted their emancipation into this life storage system many tens of thousands of years ago. The first *Grand Master* had discovered the *Oracle Machine* in a cave on *Termite* over forty thousand years ago and it had warned him of the dangers imposed by the *Xhoseti* and how to prepare for the war with them. In the end man had won the fight by collapsing the wormhole travel gate as the *Xhoseti* star ships were partially through the anomaly.

Nearly all the *Xhoseti* were destroyed when the pyramid weapons had fired, except for a small remnant of *Xhoseti* on the command ship. The partially intact space cruiser was towed to the far side of the Moon. A vote was taken to destroy or save the *Xhoseti* now safely marooned on the surface of Moon. Amazingly there was a hung vote and, in the end, he had given the order to destroy the *Xhoseti* cruiser. The ensuing explosion when the nuclear war heads had detonated was so bright that they could be seen from Earth.

Whether the *Oracle Machine* still lay undiscovered on the now decimated planet of *Termite* was yet to be determined. Man did not yet have the means to travel back to that galaxy right now but who knows what technology will be discovered in the *Guardian's* archives. Nearly all the technological advances that man had made during the rebuilding of civilisation had been under the instruction of the *Guardians*. Now man must stand alone with only *Chris* to guide them on their path through time.

The *Guardians* would be revived when the time was right for them to return to steer mankind on its new path many thousands of years from now. That in itself did not sound like man was in for a peaceful and tranquil future. So be it. If history was anything to go by, the old rivalries and conflicts would emerge as they always did; he would do what he could, but man would always be man, unpredictable and violent.

The hydrogen fuelled scram jet engines screamed as the jumper sped towards the very tip of the earth.

MOON

Soon he would be landing at the *Arctic Dome* travel port.

*

Stepping out of the shining metal craft he was greeted by seven of his most trusted acolytes.

"Greetings *Grand Master,* "

"It is good to see you all! I sense that your training has progressed at a fantastically rapid rate and that soon I will have become the apprentice," *Chris* replied to the young man standing before him. By his mannerism and bearing, he appeared to have assumed natural leadership of the seven now standing in front of him.

Sven was one of those stereo typical types from the northern region that was once known as the European nations. Standing six foot four inches tall he was an impressive figure of a man. His sky-blue eyes and thick blond hair leave nothing about his heritage in question. Bulging muscles rippled under his tight jump suit. The faint blue tinge that the *Morph-Suit* projected surrounded his body giving him an aura of godliness. He reminded *Chris* of the memory passed on by his father involving the *Norsemen* and their god of thunder *Thor*.

MOON

"*Sven*, you need to tone down your suits projection, no one is to know that you are one of the eighteenth, especially as you have the confidence of my inner circle."

"Yes *Grand Master*."

With that all of the seven's blue glow dissipated.

Ranged around him in a semicircle *Chris* inspected the seven. Starting on his left was *Khanya*, a large African with wide hips, ample padding both on her posterior and upper torso, her dreadlocks hung slightly over her dark brown eyes. Those brown intelligent eyes studied him with a slight hint of a smile; her lips were slightly ajar revealing her perfect white teeth. She would make a fantastic addition to the eighteenth; survival during the initial training phases could be fatal if one did not have enough reserves to draw on when pursuing some of the suits capabilities. Absorbing the right amount of nutrients was of paramount importance. Get it wrong and the suit will desiccate the wearer! Reserves could mean the difference between life and death.

To Khanya's left stood *Byron,* a five-foot six inch square shouldered, solemn, highly tanned man with jet black hair flecked with streaks of white along his temples; his green eyes studied *Chris* with curiosity. There was no hint of a smile on his lips; they were pursed tightly together in a flat straight line giving him an appearance of a stone statue. *Chris* couldn't decide if the man was going to attack him or embrace him. Byron wore a long dark leather overcoat that stretched down to his long brown leather riding boots; his dark appearance gave him an aura of stony menace. *Chris* stretched out his mind probe searching Byron's mind; all he encountered was a grey stone wall, a mental block of some kind.

"Very good Byron...very good indeed, I see that your training has progressed very well. You are well versed in the mental probe block."

On the extreme right of the semi-circle stood an immense Asian man that reminded *Chris* of a *Sumo* wrestler from the twentieth century. His long dark hair was tied back in a top knot emphasizing his round pleasant features; a large mouth and dark eyes complimented the smile he wore on his face when *Chris* met his gaze. He was naked apart from a large loin cloth and a long crème coloured robe which had three wooden disks running down his extended but hard midriff; the buttons were emblazoned with a serpent devouring its own tail and split the disk into a black and a white portion shaped like the symbol 'S'. *Xhaung* bowed solemnly to Chris and projected,

"Grand Master it is an honour."

"The honour is mine Xhaung, it is a pleasure to have you on the team," replied *Chris* verbally.

Next to Xhaung stood a thin gaunt stretch of a man, his short trimmed red beard bristled with life. His red flaming hair and freckled features complimented his piercing cold grey eyes. Dressed in a simple green bush jacket and with camouflage shirt, pants and brown army boots, he appeared to be ready to head out into the jungle. An interesting choice of attire thought *Chris*. *Callum* stood dead still as *Chris* looked him over, knowing that if he was to mind probe this fiery red head all he would find is a wall of flame. Callum nodded his head towards *Chris* in acknowledgment.

Standing silently next to Callum was *Posscal*, a beautiful raven haired, slender female. She almost purred with her thick Slavic accent,

"It is a pleasure to finally meet you *Grand Master*; I look forward to being of great service to you and our order."

Dressed in a light-coloured skin-tight jump suit, every detail of her lithe body was accentuated as she curtsied to *Chris*. She moved with the sensuality of a coiled snake, fluid and with purpose. *Chris* had no doubt that she could spring into action just as a poised snake

31

would prior to the fatal strike. The smile on her face was not mirrored by her strikingly hard, diamond like, azure coloured eyes.

Finally, there stood a small man almost four feet tall, his body perfectly proportioned only smaller than that of his companions. A neatly trimmed black beard surrounded his chiselled jaw line, a perfectly shaped nose and brown eyes made for the rest of his features. Old and wise seemed to be the aura that this small man projected to *Chris*. His attire was that of a simple blue cotton buttoned shirt with upturned collar, a pair of neatly tailored jeans and brown leather half boots. The small man bowed to *Chris*,

"My name is *Willow, Grand Master*; and may I just say that the only true dwarf resides not in stature but in intellect. Think small and one will remain small. Do not judge me based purely on my stature for what I lack in size I make up for in control."

With that the small man vanished only to reappear moments later hovering in a cross-legged posture with folded arms one metre above the floor. Then his appearance seemed to bend and fade, stretch and strain; there was a twisting tortured screeching noise and the dwarf no longer appeared to a small man but a *seven-foot green giant* similar to ones that the *Guardians* had grown in the Growth Pods to crush the dome uprising. The giant's green skin shone when the dome's lights reflected off its thick, almost impervious, poly-organic skin. Each muscle group on its body bulged as it stood quietly as if awaiting orders. Then it was gone and standing in its place was the small man yet again. With a small bow and a theatrical flourish of his waving hands Willow stood up and smiled at the *Grand Master*.

"Very impressive Willow...very, very impressive. Welcome to the eighteenth and the inner circle. Your talents will definitely be required, of that I am sure.

Now it is time to replenish those resources. We will all need extra water and protein for the journey to come."

With that *Chris* turned and strode across the Arctic Dome's floor, his acolytes in tight arrow head formation behind him, and headed toward the arrivals lounge and the mess hall where they could prepare themselves for the trials that would await them down below.

*

The dome's mess hall had been equipped to cater for the previous occupants of the dome, namely the grey engineering humanoids. Hatched in the *Growth Pods* and used until becoming surplus to requirements, they, with

33

the help of the *Guardian's ATS* entities, had formed the shaft running two miles deep. Each table in the mess hall was equipped with an inch-thick tube that could be extended and attached to the *Engineer's* stomach. Instead of a belly button, the engineers were grown with a direct link to their digestion pouches. They had no need to taste their food and the mouth was used purely as a means of communication. At the very far end of this sterile hall were five separate tables each equipped with four disk shaped recessed cups no larger than a dinner plate. These were designed for those with *Morph-Suit* capabilities. Walking over to the first of these tables containing the disks, *Chris* placed his hands on the plates and started to absorb the combination of protein and fluid balls that appeared above the disks. The suit allowed him to ingest the required nutrients through his hands and up the length of his arms to be stored for future use. A total mass of five kilograms was absorbed and distributed around his torso and legs. Stepping away from the plates he signalled for the rest of the group to do the same.

"Take what you need to sustain yourself for the next two days. Remember, we will need to morph air break skirts and climbing equipment. There will be no heat and very limited breathable oxygen down in the chamber."

MOON

Xhaung was the first to step up to the table. For him, ten kilograms seemed to have no effect on the girth of his torso; he just seemed to wobble slightly more. Neither did Khanya seem to change in any visible manner as she absorbed her required ten kilograms of protein and fluid. Each member of the team went through the process of absorbing their required resources with little or no effect to their outward appearance. The biggest change happened to Callum; he was no longer the slender figure of a man of ten minutes ago but now appeared to rival the physic of their local demigod Sven. *Chris* looked at Callum, studying him for a moment, and then with new found respect for his mental prowess and tenacity; gave him a nod of the head acknowledging his accomplishment. The man must have been starving prior to this feeding yet had shown no sign of his condition to anyone.

"Now that everyone has replenished their supplies we must proceed to the shaft. The hole is closing every day as the *ATS* are no longer keeping the shaft open with the ferrying of the engineering staff up and down to the chamber. We must hurry or be entombed with the *Guardians*."

Soon they were standing in front of the shaft looking down into the dark depths of what appeared to be a snake's oesophagus. Dark rings of reinforcement rimed

35

the shafts descent every three metres or so, formed naturally under the pressure waves caused by the *ATS* ships constantly travelling up and down the shaft.

Initially, one of the *ATS's* had used some form of heating on its front shield to bore the shaft into the ice and then to hollow out the spherical like shaped room in which the *Guardians* would be entombed during their stasis. After that, plastic impregnated granite had been used to line the spherical cavern and an embryonic like fluid used to insulate the gold sphere that was to house the *Guardian's* crystal stasis pods and separate it from the plastic impregnated granite shell. The stasis chamber had only recently been completed by the grey engineering staff. Now that the chamber was finished, the engineers had been sent to the *Resyk* facility, so they could be dissolved and their bodies used as a source of nourishment.

Nothing was ever wasted!

*

"Right my *seven* friends, it's time to enter the tomb, follow my lead."

Chris jumped high into the air and morphed a large shield, some two metres in diameter, to the base of his

feet. With his new shield acting as an air brake, he
dropped into the icy shaft. The air rushed past him at such
velocity that he soon found it difficult to breath; his suit
recognised the immediate asphyxiation danger and
adjusted the air intake to his lungs, adding oxygen from
the liquid in his recently absorbed rehydration pouches as
was required. The feeling of his bodily fluids being taken
from his pouches was never a pleasant one; it always felt
like he was being drained as one draws blood from a vein
but on a far more unpleasant scale. There was that initial
painful prick and then a slight vacuum induced sucking
feeling. As he fell further down the shaft, the soft white of
the ice changed to light blue then dark blue and eventually
was dark. He looked upwards and for a few seconds he
was able to get a brief glimpse of the twinkling stars above
the shaft. Then the stars were blotted out as Khanya
jumped into the shaft after him. Straight down they fell;
Chris started counting off the seconds, knowing that he
would reach the bottom in less than three minutes if he
was in total free fall. Having the *air-brake* gave him at
least double the time frame to come up with a plan on
what to do when he entered the *Guardian's* sphere. He
was waiting for the sudden change in pressure as he
exited the shaft when a rush of air blew him sideways and
he was sliding down the side of the golden sphere on a
path preordained by his soon to be entombed
grandfather. The friction generated by his shield

MOON

interacting with the gold surface caused him to pitch forward alarmingly and fall face first towards the now rapidly approaching gleaming metal surface.

"*REMOVE AIR BRAKE, MORPH SHIELD,*" Chris shouted frantically.

Rolling into a ball, *Chris* tumbled along the surface of the sphere until eventually coming to a halt and then slid down to the bottom of the structure. He mentally projected the events that had unfolded to the rest of the *seven,* so they would not be as unprepared as he was.

Standing at the bottom of the golden sphere, he took a few seconds to survey his surroundings. The walls of the sphere had a dimpled effect where the *Engineers* had installed golden spikes through the wall of the sphere and into the gelatinous like embryonic fluid. Each spike would act as a stabilisation rod, on their own useless, but together would form an anchor that could move as required yet be resistant to any sudden shock like movements. In the centre of the structure was a smaller ten metre diameter golden sphere supported at the top and bottom by a gold tube. At the base of the tube was an aperture the size of an elongated semi-circle large enough for even Khanya to pass through. It was then that the first of the *seven* started to arrive; Khanya followed his previous exploits almost exactly and shortly came skidding to a halt at his feet. She quickly composed herself and was very shortly standing by his side. Soon five more of the *seven* were standing next to him and Khanya. Looking up at the shaft entrance expecting the same antics of the small man Willow, *Chris* was surprised to see a small tube-like object protrude out of the shaft as one might imagine a turtle cautiously sticking out its head from its shell after encountering an intruder. With a plop and a slight scraping noise the tube dropped neatly down onto the top of the central sphere and slowly started to morph back into the familiar shape of the small man Willow. Standing on top of the sphere Willow gave a bow and with a flourish of his hand jumped down to be with the rest of his companions.

"Now that we are all here, some with more theatrics than others, it is time to meet the *Guardians*. Remember that they are over forty thousand years old, so may be a bit cranky. Do not ask any questions and only speak when spoken too."

With that small amount of advice given to his most trusted, *Chris* stepped into the tube. That old familiar feeling as time and space seemed as one. Within a microsecond, he was standing in the centre of the sphere that would soon be the tomb of all seven *Guardians* for the next few thousand years. Moments later his inner circle was there with him.

"Wow!" exclaimed Willow, "Now this is not what I expected, I mean talk about bigger on the inside..."

The inside of the stasis chamber was so dark that the apparently transparent shell of the sphere seemed to be a viewing platform for the entire galaxy. Stars and planets were visible to the naked eye; as soon as one focused on a particular part of the solar system or any part of the galaxy for that matter, the inquisitive owner of said focus was treated to an up-close view of that particular point of their intrigue. Water based blue planets shone under the stream of sunrays received from that particular solar system's sun. Red, dry planets gave off hazy, dusty appearances as the sand from the planet's weather system spun around its surface. The various colours of barren or fertile planets, liquid, gas or solid were vividly spellbinding.

"Yes, Willow, the effects of space and time are not the same inside the chamber as they are outside the stasis chamber," came the reply from one of the *Guardians* via the mind link intended for all present.

"It is a small gift from our ATS brethren. How they achieved such marvels in technology no one knows. We must accept such gifts with humility and charity. You see,

40

MOON

the ATS and their fellow biomechanical entities are far older than mankind, even older than the Xhoseti. What their true purpose is we have yet to discover, but over the past forty thousand years we know that mankind would not have survived without their help and guidance."

Chris wrenching his focus away from that part of the galaxy where he knew that *Termite* must exist focused his attention on his grandfather.

"It is time grandfather."

One by one each of the *Guardians* in their *Moa* like life preservation suits floated to their allotted part of the stasis chamber and came to rest in front of their respective large dark, diamond shaped crystal. The crystal appeared to be totally dormant, nothing stirred on its clean surface; it was simply just a piece of clear rock.

"We will begin the venting process in a few moments," said *Chris* to all everyone in the chamber.

There was a slow hissing noise and the sound of pressurised, heated vapour being released. An umbilical cord extended itself from the back of the *Moa* suit and latched itself to the apex of the diamond shaped crystal. Slowly the colour of the crystals started to changed colour. The process of transference lasted no more than a few

41

MOON

minutes. One by one starting on *Chris's* left the umbilical cords started to detach with a metallic clicking noise. As soon as the first cord was removed, there was a gurgling, bubbling noise as the now defunct life preservation suit started to melt and dissolve. The dark molten liquid started to drain down a hole that had appeared on the platform that the *seven* were standing. Within a few minutes only *Chris's* grandfather's suit remained. Just before the umbilical cord detached *Chris* heard his grandfather project to his mind,

"*Beware the Red ones, beware the Red...*"

Then it was over, no trace of the *Guardians* suits remained, no mind communications, no physical presence... just the now softly glowing, pulsating blue crystals.

There was a shudder; *Chris* looked up at the night sky. A film of darkness was slowly clouding over the previously star-studded ceiling. Looking down he was just in time to see the bottom tubular entrance that they had arrived through solidify and close making a seamless surface.

MOON

"*Right! That must be our cue to get out while we still can,*" stated *Chris* calmly via the mind link to the others.

Standing under the overhead aperture, *Chris* wondered how they were going to get up that high and get out when he experienced that silky feeling again. Time and space appeared as one.

When *Chris* realised where he was, he gave an involuntary stagger only to be caught on his left by Sven and on his right by Khanya as they travelled up the shaft on what appeared to be a large speeding disk of ice. He could hear the shaft closing beneath them as they sped up towards the surface; the cracking and crushing sounds beneath their feet felt like they were riding a speeding glacial type of tidal wave. The immense power of the upwards thrust almost knocked him to his knees. If he and the rest of the *seven* were not tightly embraced he was sure that they would all be individually pushed downwards and on to their faces. Standing together they were stronger, stronger than even the force of this colossal gravitational force trying to crush them.

The disk shot out of the shaft and then shattered, sending shards of now dissolving ice high into the air. Each shard melted harmlessly away, before being dissipated by the billowing wind.

43

MOON

Seven voices almost instantaneously shouted,

"*SHIELD*" as the inner members fell roughly onto the snow-covered ground.

Chris had projected an overhead air-brake disk that slowed his vertical expulsion velocity and now acted as a parachute to bring him down, making a soft landing on the snow.

In the distance the faint shape of the Arctic Dome could be made out and without a word they headed straight for it. Soon there was no trace of the stasis chamber's shaft as the snow started to cover any remaining trace of the now collapsed exit.

Entering the dome, it became apparent that they would need to leave almost immediately. On the arrivals screen, in large red letters, were the words

EVACUATE...DESTRUCTION...IMMINENT...

EVACUATE...DESTRUCTION...IMMINENT...

EVACUATE...DESTRUCTION...IMMINENT...

TIME TO DESTRUCTION...30...SECONDS

29 SECONDS

Chris and the *seven* ran for the jumper which was thankfully still were they left it. As they entered the jumper *Chris* caught a last glance of the countdown.

5 SECONDS

The jumper lifted off, the hydrogen fuelled rockets screaming in protest at being slammed into overdrive. They were just three hundred metres away when a blinding white ball erupted from the centre of the dome and started to spin. The entire dome started to creak and shriek as the superstructure was sucked into the centre of the brilliant white ball. Within minutes the whole of the Arctic Dome was no more. Silence deafened his ears; the more he strained to hear, the more nothing he heard. It was as if a vacuum had replaced the space where the dome had been.

Where the arctic dome had once stood lay a vast hole. Soon the snow started to cover and fill the hole, covering the snowy landscape. As they watched, the snow storm seemed to intensify and soon the flurry of snow had covered the entire area with clean white frozen snow drops.

The dome had simply vanished.

MOON

Turning to his companions, *Chris* waited for someone to speak. Eventually Willow broke the silence,

"Well that went well. I suppose it was all part of the plan! I mean that was close. Do you think the shaft would have closed and entombed us if were had not acted so quickly?"

"Don't worry little man; I am sure that the *Grand Master* would have carried you to the surface if you couldn't hold yourself together," retorted Callum a sneer distorting his features.

"You just leave Willow alone Callum. Not everyone can be as outwardly emotionless as you," said Khanya springing to Willow's defence.

"Thank you Khanya, but I don't need your help with the small-minded quips of the likes of the ginger over there. I do however appreciate you having my back. And make no mistake when the time comes I will repay the favour," Willow raised a thumb to his nose, waggled his raised fingers at Callum and stuck out his tongue.

"Real mature you little mite. It's a good job the boss is here to stop me from getting all flames and brimstone on your small ass," Callum crossed his arms and glared at the little man.

MOON

The rest of the *seven* continued the journey in silence as the jumper sped on towards City One.

Chris, looking at Callum's body language did not like what he saw. They were a team, but it looked like some personality clashes needed to be resolved. They could not have any discord between themselves if they encountered an enemy. It would be even worse for them if they ever found themselves up against an *Xhoseti Warrior*.

*

47

MOON

XHOSETJ

MOON

MOON

TUNNELS

Chapter Four

Moon

Xhoseti Tunnels

Xhespo scurried away from the generator hall with its life-giving resource, one quickly dispatched white rat. Careful not to deplete this limited and valuable carbon-based life form, *Xhespo* chose only the biggest and most damaged of these rodents. They were so easy to snatch; all grouped together at the very peak of this man-made structure, not even a challenge. They grouped together for protection, leaving the youngest and weakest in the centre of their packs. This was exactly what *Xhespo* wanted, the biggest and juiciest.

Xhosepo's memory took him back a few hundred years, back to that dreaded moment when the worm gate had closed on his star-cruiser, the ensuing helpless placement of himself and the crew on the surface of the *Moon;* and then the explosion.

Xhespo's mandibles shook in agitation. Anger filled *Xhespo's* mind; revenge would be theirs.

Once stranded on the Moon, *Xhespo* had given the order to dig and dig fast. His loyal and faithful brood had dug until their mandibles and claws broke, doing so knowing that they would be the first to pay the ultimate price when resources were depleted. They gave their lives willingly. Of the hundred souls or so that had scrabbled out the tunnels straight down in to the depths of the Moon, *Xhespo was* the only remaining *Xhoseti* left on this barren rock. They had tunnelled as fast as was *Xhoseti* possible before *Xhespo* ignited the plasma grenades to seal the tunnel's exit point from their ship. A short while later a huge explosion could be heard and part of the tunnel closest to the surface had been subject to such intense heat that the collapsed rock had been turned to molten lava. Then, under the vacuum and chill of space, in short order it had turned to hard, obsidian like glass.

As they tunnelled further and further into the depths of the Moon's core, it was clear that this hunk of rock was still active. The tunnels became warmer and warmer the further they dug. It would appear that the Moon's constant struggle with the gravitational pull of the Earth trying to tear it apart and with the continual effort to resist being torn apart was creating tremendous frictional energy which was in turn heating the core of the Moon.

51

Then one day one of the *Xhoseti* diggers fell through the bottom of one of the tunnels that was being scraped out and fell into a large spherical chamber. The sphere for want of a better word appeared to be manmade. They all scurried into the chamber, eager to find the owner of such a structure and devour it (or preferably them) in order to quell their own hunger. Instead they found nothing, just an empty chamber, smooth to the touch. *Xhespo* stood up on his back legs searching for something of any value in this huge cavernous space. Nothing...wait what was that soft red glow coming from the corner of the cavern.

A red glowing fungus coated the walls of the chamber. *Xhespo* scurried hurriedly towards the red glowing patch high up on the ceiling. As *Xhespo* scampered along the smooth spherical cavern's interior, soft red glowing claw prints indicating the path *Xhespo* had travelled appeared behind him. Soon the whole sphere was alight with a red glow as the rest of his brood explored their potential new home. The red fungus seemed to greet their new guests with glowing red enthusiasm. Each time an *Xhoseti* warrior touched a part of the sphere the red fungus coated their claws, then their mandibles and within minutes their entire bodies.

Soon all of the *Xhoseti* were coated with the red glowing fungus.

52

MOON

One of his underlings regurgitated some digestive fluids onto a patch of the red fungus and it rapidly became a small, but nutritious, thick viscous like mass. The underling sucked it up with its proboscis and screeched information about this newly found resource to the others. On mass the *Xhoseti* survivors set about dissolving the red fungus and digesting it. *Xhespo* stood and watched them gorge themselves. Soon all the fungus on the cavern's surface had been consumed. The only fungus that remained was the coating of the exoskeletons of those who had scampered through the fungus. Each surviving member of his crew now glowed with a soft red light. The brightness varied from *Xhoseti* to *Xhoseti* depending on their size and stature.

At first there was no reaction to the fungus, the *Xhoseti* exoskeleton being extremely tough and virtually impervious to the perils of space; both radiation and the crushing effects of full vacuum were easily shrugged off. That being said, the fungus too was a hardy entity, having survived the rigors of space and time with nothing for nutrition but the minerals leeched from the rocks to survive on. Soon the fungus's roots drove deeper and deeper into the hapless *Xhoseti* shells and slowly started to drain the insectoid horde of its nutrients.

Xhespo recognised this slow working but inevitable threat to his crew and issued orders for each of his crew to groom the other. Soon they set about regurgitating their digestive fluids on each other and sucking up the nutritious gelatinous mass that remained. All was going well and the fungus seemed to have been cleared when one of his more senior crew keeled over dead, red fungus growing out of its eyes.

"DESTROY THAT HUSK...BE FAST...FEAST...FEAST," *Xhespo* shrieked.

Immediately five of his crew set about the task. *Xhespo* stood back watching.

One by one his crew succumbed to this growing infestation; each time the result was the same. After a few weeks all except *Xhespo* were dead.

Having retreated back up to the hole in which they had first stumbled through and into this predator like red fungus' lair, *Xhespo* looked down upon the remains of the last of the *Xhoseti* crew. Exoskeletons lay scattered about the base of the cavern in various stages of agony, red fungus covered their remains. Slowly they were being dissolved and the red glowing fungus was creeping back around the spherical shaped cavern. With the red glow starting to return to the walls of the sphere it was starting to resemble the inside of an animal's digestive pouch, the red fungus's tendrils reaching out testing the air for any signs of resources, eerily always pointing in *Xhespo's* direction. Occasionally tiny puffs of spores could be seen being ejected into the nearby volume of space and soon new fungus roots started to sprout from wherever the spores had landed.

Xhespo looked down at his claws and was horrified to see a slight reddish glow on their very tips. Hastily he regurgitated some digestive fluids on them dissolving the red fungus.

Scrabbling in panic back up the tunnel the now deceased *Xhoseti* crew had dug...*Xhespo fled*.

*

Xhespo scuttled along the tunnel not caring were it led. A previously unnoticed fork here, a left and a left...lost *Xhespo* stopped and waited for normality to return.

"What is that humming ssound?"

A faint pulsating tremor could be felt through the ceiling of the tunnel that *Xhespo* was crouching in. The tunnel was larger than the ones the crew had dug. Standing up on hind legs, *Xhespo* could just touch the

55

ceiling. There were reinforcement rings every three metres along this tunnel, definitely not *Xhoseti* made, but then, by whom?

"*Humanss!*" *Xhespo* hissed.

"*They musst pay...*"

Slowly *Xhespo* crawled low to the floor of the tunnel as a predator would stalk its prey, slowly creeping towards this potential source of nutrition.

The vibrations became more intense the closer to the manmade building *Xhespo* got. Lights could be seen at the end of the tunnel. The air shimmered and shook with the immense amount of energy being discharged around the entrance to this room. Cautiously, looking at the walls of the tunnel *Xhespo* realised that this must be one of the service tunnels used to remove spent production, by-products or simply a Moon dust removal chute.

Shaking the dust off its exoskeleton, *Xhespo* slowly snuck into the generator hall, the effects of the generator's gravitational pull immediately trying to separate *Xhespo* from the floor it was standing on. Claws dug deep...slowly move away from the pull...exoskeleton being tugged at...separation imminent. It was then that *Xhespo* noticed the red fungus again,

56

"Will this pesst never go away?"

Xhespo scampered up the sides of the building away from the gravitational pull of the generators and clung to one of the beams holding up the superstructure.

"Only one thing left to do if I am to rid us of this pesst, shed thiss sshell."

Excreting a sticky gel from its mandibles; *Xhespo* started to join itself to the beam. *Xhespo* started weaving a sticky cocoon like structure around its body. Soon the *Xhoseti* was encased in a soft gelatinous sac. Within a few minutes the sac had hardened to a dark reflective sphere.

Xhespo settled in the sac and waited. Soon the digestive juices in the sac would dissolve its hard chitinous like exterior and a new one would form, cleaning *Xhespo* of this accursed plague of a fungus.

*

A few days later the now considerably lighter shade of brown sac started moving. A dark shape could barely be made out inside the cocoon. Within minutes a tear started to form on the bottom of the spherical like sac. Slowly a soft semi-transparent claw poked its way out of the sac and soon the rest of the newly formed soft exoskeleton that belonged to *Xhespo* started to emerge.

57

MOON

With a soft squelching sound, the whole body of the newly formed *Xhoseti Queen* dropped from the sac suspended by a tendon like attachment. *Xhespo* hung in the air of the generator room waiting for her exoskeleton to harden.

Above the sac the red fungus stirred, aware of the activity taking place below where it had attached itself to the sphere.

Sensing that the opportunity to infest and ultimately consume the unwilling host below, it stretched out its tendrils seeking the presence of the source of disturbance. Small puffs of spores ejected from the tip of the tendrils and started to rapidly spread down the sides of the now elongating sac.

Xhespo, sensing that the fungus was still near, wriggled and struggled to free herself from the tendon tying her to the sac. Her shell was not hardening quick enough and each time she tried to raise her claw upwards to cut through the cord, the appendage would collapse down to her side with the lack of a solid surface to pump the required pressure into the tubes that powered her motions. In a panic, she could make out the progress of the red fungus slowly expelling spores that clung to the sides of the now elongated sac, she hung there waiting for the end. The heavier she became, the longer the sac stretched. The fungus sensed that its quarry was winning

58

the race to escape and seemed to double its efforts to grow and spread down the sides of the now thinning sac. The very extremities of the red fungus's attachment to the generator halls superstructure turned a bleached white colour as nutrients were sucked out of them and sent flooding to where they were needed for the reproduction of the new spores. They were close, so close...just a few more seconds and the resource could be infected.

Xhespo twisted and shook, the sac extended even more, the red fungus was almost upon her, all that effort to be rid of the parasite only to fail.

Xhespo gave one last desperate swing of her claw upwards in a slashing arc and was rewarded with a tearing sound as the cord gave way. *Xhespo* dropped down onto the almost gravitational inert neutral space of the walkway. Even here though, the effects of the generators gravity started to pull her upwards and towards one of the gigantic spinning balls of light. Her shell was hardening at a rapid rate but just not quick enough; she could feel the sucking effect of the machine slowly tugging and ripping her exoskeleton from her inner chambers. A tearing noise filled her mind as the exoskeleton hardened and was sheared by the pull of gravity. Just when she thought it was all over, there was an additional gravitational pull of another nearby generator, then nothing, no pull...no

59

shear...no tearing. Drifting slowly down to the walkway in the eye of the gravitational pulls, *Xhespo* slowly descended. Ten minutes later she landed on the cold hard plastic surface of the walkway grating that was making imprints on her now almost completely hardened exoskeleton.

Lying on her back she inspected each of her extremities for the red fungus, then her mandibles.

"Cleanss!" she blurted out.

Staring up at the ceiling she had recently been attached to; the red fungus glowed bright red in what could only be described as frustration.

It was then, whilst lying in her back that she noticed the red fungus change course, no longer intent on pursuing her as a source of nutrition. She saw what the fungus had sensed the animal like beings further along the ceiling. Some sort of mammal, white with hideously deformed features, had gathered in a pocket of air that had floated to the top of the generator hall.

The rats seemed to be covered in some sort of white dust.

The red fungus slowly, with purpose and intent, crept towards the huddled group of white rats. When the

60

fungus reached the pocket of air it stopped, pausing for a moment as if testing this new environment in which the recently identified prey resided. Slowly it extended its tendrils, poking and testing the air. Then, with a burst of newly found energy, it rapidly surged forward towards the now panicked group of squeaking rats. The fungus seemed to glow a brighter red in the low oxygenated atmosphere and with renewed energy sent spores into the air, laying down its minute fungal roots as it spread towards the huddled group.

Just as the fate of the Moon dust cover rodents seemed sealed, the fungus bloomed and expanded, rising several centimetres into the air, glowing bright red and imploded. What remained was a rapidly fading dull red mass of oozing gelatinous like porridge. Outside the air bubble, the fungus quickly severed its extremity tendrils closest to the air pocket and seemed to shrink back towards the now fungus encrusted *Xhoseti* sac.

The largest and most hideously deformed rat in the pack hesitantly approached the thick porridge like substance which only moments ago was intent on devouring the rat slowly and painfully. Then the rat pounced sinking its large deformed canines into the thick oozing mass. The rat, expecting a fight, shook its head

61

back and forth as a dog would do to it should the roles be reversed. *Nothing happened!*

The rat stopped shaking its adversary and tore off a small bite of the now dead fungus. Squeaking its delight, it turned towards the others in the huddled group of rodents as if beckoning them to join it. Soon the small group of rodents were all scrambling to get at the nutrient rich gel that had made itself available for them to feast on.

Xhespo, now with exoskeleton fully hardened, knew that this was an opportunity that could not be missed. As the rats feasted on the remains of the fungus, she crept slowly up the wall of the generator room, avoiding the gravitational pull of the generators, and snuck into the air bubble. One of the rats turned to see *Xhespo* just about to pounce on one of the churning mass of white bodies and let out a call of alarm. As one, the rats turned on *Xhespo* and deformed mouths ajar in a snarl surged towards her. *Xhespo* twisted to one side and with a flick of her claw snatched the closest of the rodents and sped out of the air pocket. The rat struggled to regain its freedom, squirming and biting at the claw in which *Xhespo* held the doomed creature. Soon the struggling rodent was gasping for air and with a choking, gasping splutter, went limp. *Xhespo* put the now asphyxiated rodent down on the grating of the walkway and regurgitated her digestive juices over the

62

body of her soon to be absorbed nutritious snack. Soon she was using her proboscis to suck up the rapidly dissolving body of the rodent.

Returning to the tunnel entrance where he had entered the generator room, *Xhespo* cautiously poked her head into the tunnel looking for the red fungus. Seeing no trace of the fungus she crept into the tunnel retracing her steps.

Reaching a fork in the tunnel she could not decide which way to take. Slowly taking her time she waited and listened.

The left tunnel seemed quiet, inviting, then came the smell. The smell of her dead and consumed crew.

"Not that way thenss."

Entering the right fork, she could feel a slight vibration resonating through the tunnels walls. The half metre tunnel was barely big enough for her to squeeze through. Oddly the size reminded her of the tunnels her crew had dug when they were escaping from the *Xhoseti* space cruiser. It would appear as if one of her kind had been here before and scraped out this section of the shaft. After a few minutes of crawling along the shaft it opened up into a larger tunnel. This one, a metre and a half in

63

diameter, appeared to have been cut into the bedrock with some kind of laser weapon. Every three metres there were rings that rimmed the tunnel walls reminding *Xhespo* of an animal's oesophagus. She continued cautiously; the vibrations becoming more intense.

Then suddenly the vibrations stopped; silence descended on the tunnel. When the tunnel had vibrated there seemed to be life in the walls. Now there was nothing but the cold emptiness of space.

Xhespo was alone, the last of her kind. Now she must find resources to consume and impregnate if the *Xhoseti* were to survive.

Slowly and cautiously she continued down the tunnel.

*

MOON

EARTH

COUNCIL

MEETING

MOON

Chapter Five

Earth

Kilimanjaro

Council Building

During the previous world war back in the twenty second century, many dormant volcanoes erupted into life as the Earth's seismic activity increased with the detonation of so many nuclear warheads. If it was not for the *Guardians* and *ATS* entities that had provided the seven *Domes* into which the genetically selected portion of humanity had been ushered, there would be no human beings left to populate the planet. Approximately ninety nine percent of mankind perished in the ensuing ash fallout.

The devastation and radiation caused by the nuclear weapons destroyed most of the cities and factories. Tsunamis and volcanic eruptions had added to the devastation, but the blanket of ash that had enveloped the stratosphere, blocking out nearly all of the sun's life-giving rays, had put an end to any chance of photosynthesis essential to all plant life on the surface. Nearly all plant-based life forms perished. There were however some very basic hardy forms of plant-based life that had survived. One of these hardy life forms was the bioluminescent algae that had flourished to such an extent that it had to be eradicated so the repopulation of plant-based life forms could be reintroduced. Once the defence ring had cleaned the atmosphere most of the algae perished when exposed to the sun's radiation. The dead algae remains acted as fertiliser and helped to re-sow the planet with new vegetation.

Now during the shifting of tectonic plates, one of the volcanoes to erupt catastrophically was Mount Kilimanjaro which had stood on the plains of the then Republic of Kenya. Having remained without a major eruption for over three hundred thousand years, Mount Kilimanjaro was ready for a climate eruption changing event. When the Earth shook, and the ground heaved, a crack appeared deep down in the bowels of the African country's tectonic plates, resulting in a gigantic build up of magma. At first, lava spewed a mile high from the centre of the stratovolcano mountain then it erupted violently. As the pressure built up and could no longer be contained, the base of the mountain cracked and sheared. Then the whole mountain was shot straight up, sending billions of tonnes of previously created pyroclastic lava into the surrounding countryside. The release of pressure with the removal of the cap acted much like the eruption of an over shaken bottle of champagne - an initial loud bang and release of fluid and gas only to carry on spilling over until the previously contained energy had dissipated.

Kibo, Mawenzi and Shria volcanic cones lay in ruin down on the African savannah. Soon all three of the volcanic cones were liquefied as the heat of the molten flowing lava engulfed and slowly dissolved them. After the cataclysmic event had subsided and the Earth was plunged into darkness, the flat topped, now hardened lava mountain remained undiscovered until the early twenty sixth century.

Today imbedded on the top volcanically created plateau, the translucent birds nest like crystal bowl structure of the *Council's Dome;* resplendent in all its shining glory, acted as a beacon of light and could be seen shining across the savannah for many hundreds of miles. All who first approached the many faceted crystal grown structure marvelled at its magnificence. The crystal dome of the council could be seen as a brightly lit bowl even from space, day or night made no difference to the radiance of this impressive homogeneous crystalline structure.

Powered by a shaft running six miles down into the Earth's magma, latent heat was turned directly into electricity via thermal electrical generators. As long as the magma remained so did the supply of electricity.

*

Chris was late again; he made a mental note chastising himself, when the council meeting was over he would have to put more effort into paying attention to his calendar reminders, but for now it was all he could do to contain his excitement. In a few minutes he would present a paper outlining the latest proposal he had drafted to upgrade the energy facility on the Moon.

Rushing past the statue like figure of the entrance guard *Chris* powered his *Morph-Suit* to aid his speed. The suit complied with his request and hydraulic cylinders in his legs were formed and pressurised, giving him the additional power required to walk as fast as any man could sprint.

The corridor he was powering down was filled with light, a side effect of the crystal walls and ceilings which gave off a slight pulsation as the thermally generated energy surged through the crystalline bird nest structure. He was nearing the end of the corridor when a guard stepped in front of him to bar his entrance to the Council chamber.

"Halt sir, you are too late! The Council is in session and no one is to enter."

Chris looked at the red leather jumpsuit clad man, his hand out stretched, palm facing him. The guard's stance indicating a no compromise, no entry attitude. *Chris* then mentally instructed his suit to make him invisible.

"Wait...Halt! What the...where did he go!" exclaimed the guard in astonishment.

Chris slipped past the frozen man and continued on his way to the central podium in the middle of the room's floor.

Still cloaked and powered by the hydraulic cylinders in his legs, he was just able to jump the five metres or so up onto the now rising podium stage. Standing silently to one side of the podium, he watched as council member Jeremy stood at the lectern waiting for the stage to complete its upward journey. The tall slender man with wispy white hair, white stubble beard, a hooked, somewhat crooked nose and darting blue eyes, fidgeted with his hands. Sometimes rubbing them together, sometimes wringing them but always active. A faint sneer touched his lips, dark tobacco stained crooked teeth could

70

just be made out every time the sneer almost became a smile.

The stage came to a halt with a slight creak and hiss as the hydraulically powered lifting mechanism locked into place.

The rest of the now seven major cities' delegates filed into the room and headed to their allotted cubicles.

*

During the fallout years mankind had been protected and nurtured by the *Guardians* and the *ATS* biomechanical entities. Huge Dome force fields had been projected and powered by the *ATS*. When the atmosphere had been cleared by the planetary defence ring's extractors, the shields had come down and man and beast were released back onto the planet's surface to procreate and build as they saw fit.

As per any previous controlling establishment, the illusion of freedom of thought and expression had to be maintained; the populace was always under the watchful eye and guidance of the *Guardians*. Guilds had been established, religious and political sects encouraged but all under the subtle influence of the *Guardians*. If things looked like they were not going according to the

Guardian's carefully laid out plans, the perpetrators of the anti-establishment leaders were visited by *Chris* and under direct instruction made to change their point of view. Normally a vision of the *Xhoseti* rounding up human children to be used as slave labour or simply being dissolved by the *Xhoseti* digestive juices before being sucked up, was enough to remind the traitor of how the *Guardians* saved the human race and why they should respect the *Guardian's* point of view.

*

Chris still cloaked, surveyed the council members that were now reclining comfortably in their respective booths. The brightly lit chamber was filled with the twenty-one council members all dressed according to their guilds or sects recognised attire. The workers' guild members were wearing orange jumpsuits and sporting uncut flowing hair of all lengths and colours. Their respective city number emblazoned on the front and back of the jumpsuit that each member of the worker guild wore.

The religious cast wore yellow robes and yellow sandals; they too had the number of their city embossed on the front and back of their robes. The political class were more formal and wore three buttoned black suits, white upturned collared shirts with thin black ties and a black bowler hat resting on their shaven heads. The number of their respective city was tattooed in white letters on their left and right cheeks.

Each of the seven major cities was required to send a representative of the religious, political and working guilds to the council meetings.

The design of the seven cities habitation structures were all of a similar construction and the inner city structures all resembled one another. The initial tubular structures used to house the thousands of survivors in the domes were duplicated and placed strategically around the first habitation. Each subsequent sky habitation tube was linked to the central habitation tube every three hundred metres up its vertical exterior with a horizontal sky tunnel. Here was where the markets stores had been established, anything manufactured or grown outside the habitation tubes could be traded or bartered for in these tunnels.

As the human population expanded, the need for more habitation tubes increased and rapidly additional tubes were constructed and linked to each other. As the cities grew the need for more and more power to run the cities light, water and sanitation systems overwhelmed the central wind tunnel's power generating capabilities. The *Resyk* centres were running at full capacity and any additional need for recycling would strain the already overloaded machinery. All human and animal remains were ground up in the *Resyk* vats and along with discarded plant matter turned into a nutritious grey paste that was available in the market stalls.

This source of protein, fibre and vitamins was available to all without having to be traded or bartered for. No one would ever need to go hungry as long as the *Resyk* vats could be powered.

*

Standing at the lectern Jeremy started his carefully prepared speech.

"As the elected representative of all the guilds and sects for all *seven cities* I open with the customary greeting.

Hail the Guardians who have saved us from the Xhoseti and peace be upon all the chosen who came from the Domes."

A good start thought *Chris* still cloaked.

"And now to business...

74

MOON

As you all know our major concern is, as it always is, *power*. As we grow and start to take back our rightful place as rulers of the *Earth* there is always the question of where will we get more power?

The *Guardians* have forbidden the use of cheap readily available fossil fuels. *Yes...*I know that they pollute the environment and will cause some form of climatic change. We know that some of this pollution will not always be of a positive nature, but we can learn from the mistakes of our ancestors. The fuel is there, some of it already bubbling out of the ground, made available during the last tectonic plate upheavals. Why not use it? *It's just sitting there!*

As to who will own the rights to this new resource, well that is what we need to vote on right now, right here, in this chamber."

There was a murmur of consent amongst the political class representatives and some of dissent amongst the worker class. The religious class remained silent as normal.

After a short consultation between themselves using the communication links in each booth, the working-class guilds stood as one. Their apparent leader, a large man with a grey beard and short neatly trimmed hair, cleared his throat indicating that he wished to speak.

"You have the floor Miguel of the *Workers' Guild*."

"Thank you *vice*-chairman.

Firstly, we feel that without the *Grand Master* being present to voice the *Guardians* opinion regarding this subject, your motion amounts to near treason and we believe that you will be held accountable for this action at some future date.

Secondly, who is going to design and build all these new wonderful process and power plants? We will of course be called upon to do so, and as such should own the rights to them. That is of course, if they are given the *Guardian's* blessing to proceed.

Thirdly, this is not why we are here; the agenda clearly stipulated that we are here to discuss the design and construction of the proposed new source of energy for the Moon's generator plants. Where is the *Grand Master* so we can proceed with this agenda? This is after all the only reason why we have all gathered here in this magnificent building on this day,"

Miguel looked around at his fellow guild members who gave him the thumbs up and nodded their heads in agreement.

"Well the *Grand Master* is not here, so as vice chairman, I have the authority and power to change the agenda as I see fit," retorted Jeremy.

Chris having seen and heard enough de-cloaked.

Silence filled the room as the *Grand Master's* presence became noticed.

"Why are you all so quiet? *Cat got your tongue?*" asked Jeremy.

It was then that he felt *Chris's* hand on his shoulder.

"*Oh...*"

"Thank you, mister vice-chairman, I will proceed with the real reason we are here."

Jeremy left the lectern, moved quietly to the edge of the platform, and slumped down into his allotted chair, vice chairman emblazoned on the headrest.

"The *Guardians* have been generous again in the sharing of their technology. What they have revealed to me is a new form of energy generation. Like all high

77

energy power projects, it is not without its drawbacks, but I believe that the benefits far outweigh the risks. If the project is implemented correctly and to the exact specifications that I have laid out in the dossier you now have access to on your interface panels, then it will succeed, and man will no longer need to find alternative sources of power. This power generation plant will solve all of your current power shortage issues and still have surplus energy for future expansion.

Jeremy rose from his chair and blurted out his objections,

"And where will the political and religious classes be in all this? What will their responsibilities be?"

"To answer your questions, mister *vice*-chairman, they will both have the same responsibilities as they have at present. Help the worker guilds to deliver the materials and manpower required to successfully construct the power plant. Look after their mental and spiritual wellbeing, represent them to the greatest of your abilities,"

Chris paused for effect and then continued,

"The power generation plant has been divided into various sections of responsibility; there are electrical power systems, mechanical equipment requirements, structural and civil integrity design work sections, the list goes on and on. I will not bore you with the details of the inner workings of the power plant. That level of detail has been transmitted to your various cities' guilds to be resourced and manufactured as defined in the detailed design documents. We have a tight schedule to be adhered to as the soon to be overloaded power plant on the Moon is due to have its maintenance outage in the next five months.

When the new power plant is up and running the maintenance schedule will be a thing of the past and the existing power plant can be put into storage, moth-balled so to speak. It will only be revived should there be an energy crisis. Now are there any questions?"

"*Grand Master*," City One's Workers' Guild representative rose from his booth to address *Chris*.

"Yes Jose, you have a question?" replied *Chris*.

"I do *Grand Master*, now that the *ATS* entities have all disappeared, how are we to ferry the components to the Moon for construction?"

"That is a good question. Initially the ground works will setup by automated bots. They are already starting with the new dome habitations for the workers to live in. Work will be started and completed on the Moon. If possible, all the required building materials will be mined from the Moon itself. Anything else that is required will be sourced firstly from the asteroid belt, then as a last resort flown up from earth. All prefabricated machinery will be modularised for assembly on the Moon. The *Guardian's* data base also yielded a blue print for a slingshot design that will be established on the defence ring which can be adapted for terrestrial use as well.

Initially all terrestrial prefabricated modules will be propelled via the catapult system into the atmosphere then hydrogen oxygen scram jet propulsion will be used to escape the earth's gravitational pull and power the cargo the rest of the way to the docking bays on the defence ring.

As many modules as can be assembled will be. They will be hooked up or connected in the docking bays and then ejected via the slingshot to the receiving catchment funnel on the Moon. The only limitation will be the size of the modules as the access tunnels into the habitation and generator domes can only be as large as the tunnel bots themselves."

"That sounds fantastical and may even be plausible, but as you know we will always have our doubts and until we go over the plans and establish design committees, I for one am sceptical. We will await your designs and once the habitations are complete send the required staff there to help with construction. I presume that the mining operations will be carried out by mining bots as well?" questioned Jose.

"Correct, now thank you councillor member Jose.

Are there any more questions?

If not, then this council meeting is closed. Please have your engineers read the design documents carefully and send you as the head of your respective guilds any queries that they may have. I am sure we will have a few stumbling blocks to be overcome, but that is to be expected. For your information mining vessels are already on their way to the asteroid belt to search for water and other materials that may be required to make the Moon habitation a success.

I thank you all for attending.

Meeting closed!"

Meeting adjourned, the podium platform started to descend and soon had reached ground level. By the time *Chris* had reached the ground, all of the council members had filed out of the room, some in deep discussion with

81

others of their class, the religious class all clad in yellow were silent. Indignation could be heard emanating from the political members, bowler hats bobbing up and down in vehement agreement with each other about the indignity they had just been subject too.

Excitement radiated from the worker class representatives. There was a feeling of purpose, a feeling of pride. Mankind had a new goal; political policies had been pushed to one side and all that mattered now was to start and complete this new challenging project.

Councillor Jose turned to some of the closest Worker Guild members,

"Councillors...I think we need to have a member only meeting between ourselves. If the Workers Guild is to achieve this fantastical sounding power generation plant on the Moon, then we must get organised. What say you?"

A few of the orange jumpsuit clad men and women gathered closer to Jose. Looking at each other they nodding in agreement,

"We think that there needs to be work flow chart and responsibility matrix documents produced just to start with;" came the response from Cathy, leader of City Three's Worker Guild.

"If we are to succeed then clear and precise roles must be established. No city should be left out of the manufacturing process. The only way to efficiently manufacture the components will be to assign sections of fabrication and design to each city. Let's start today. I will arrange a meeting room and instruct our engineers to fly here immediately," she continued.

"Good idea Cathy, I will get my design engineering team to fly up as well. I suggest you all get the rest of your team members here as soon as possible so we can establish our strengths and weaknesses to assign the various tasks to each city," said Jose to the other council members now huddled around him.

"Remember though, the *Grand Master* will still have to approve our design proposals and manufacturing allotment factories for each city," stated Cathy, then settled down to draw up her work flow proposal hoping to win the bid for the majority of the main shuttle components.

*

MOON

XHOSETJ

MOON

MOON

POWER

PLANT

85

Chapter Six

Moon

Power Plant

Construction Site:

Luke, standing on the viewing deck where he normally took his lunch gazed out of the reinforced polycarbonate composite porthole. As per his routine he had completed his inspection rounds earlier this morning. Being an early riser he general found that he had a lot of free time to amuse himself with. As he stared out of the viewing window his thoughts went back to the strange insect like creature he had seen the other day in the generator hall. What was that scurrying thing? Before he could dwell on the subject his mind was distracted by the events taking place out on the Moon's surface.

The view from up here was spectacular, white and flat for miles with of course the occasional small rock. He could see the habitation *construction-bots* traversing the Moon's surface heading towards their allotted grid coordinates. The habitation domes were to form the outer ring of the new power station.

Each of the seven domes would be used to house the work force that would be instrumental in the assembly

86

of the sections of the power generator machines before being connected together in the main power plant building. The domes would also store the completed modules sent from the defence ring and any other materials required to construct the power plant.

Each dome would be responsible for the completion of their city's engineering design portion of the project. The design and construction of each section had been carefully allocated to the individual city by the *Grand Master* based on the city's expertise and available resources.

The seven-dome *construction-bots* had reached their grid locations and stood silent awaiting the command to start digging.

*

Sitting in front of his computer console, Hendrik, now aware that the construction bots were awaiting his order to continue, ran through his check list. The command and control room resided deep down in the bowels of the existing power generator plant's structure. To compensate for the lack of viewing windows, each wall inside the control room was covered with viewing screens able to focus on any individual construction activity as was required. At present the walls showed an overall

87

proposed plot plan of the overall project on the main wall. The other walls were each dedicated to the seven construction robot activities.

"*Bot-one* grid location set, variation from grid coordinates five inches, *well within tolerance!*

Check...all green.

Fuel levels steady at ninety seven percent.

Check...all green.

Communication check, ping to *bot-one*, response ping confirmed.

Check...all green."

He continued down the list for each of the construction robots.

"Damn, bot-seven is off by a few metres. Moving *construction-bot-seven* manually. Hold on, will just be a few minutes,"

Hendrik pushed a button on his desk and a joy stick rose out of its surface. Typing in the manual override code he started to move the construction vehicle to the correct location.

"*Construction-bot-seven* move to grid location complete."

Running through the check list again for *bot-seven* he gave the check list the all clear.

"Have a look at the check list Teri," Hendrik turned to his co-worker sitting at the other desk in the control room.

"Looks good to me," she replied handing the clip board back to him.

"Well don't just say it, sign it, you know how the quality control plan gets audited!"

Sighing in exasperation Teri took back the clip board and scribbled her signature on each of the construction-bot's check list sheets.

"Here it is. *You stickler!*"

Ignoring her mocking tone Hendrik continued,

"Right, next phase. Time to start digging," he pulled out his access card and placed it into the slot provided on his keyboard. Teri did the same, typing in her password and security employment number.

"Right let's crank this sucker up!" said Teri a bit too theatrically.

Hendrik typed in the command for the construction bots to begin the next phase of the habitation construction process.

As one, the construction robots began opening up their upright cylindrical bodies. Apertures opened two thirds of the way up the cylindrical bodies and five equidistantly spaced stabilisation arms extended out from each of the robots. The extended arms gave the *construction-bots* the appearance of an alien five-legged spider waiting to pounce.

At the very tip of the arms were sharp pointed dark spikes. Each one slowly lowered itself onto the lunar surface and started to vibrate the sharp protrusions into the ground searching for solid bedrock.

Within twenty minutes all of the spikes had reached the hard bedrock that would form the anchorage platform of the main construction machinery.

"All stop.

Scanning quality of anchor positions," said Hendrik out loud.

After a few minutes Hendrik had flicked over the density reports that appeared on his screen.

"Check...all green.

We are good to proceed with anchorage connections."

Teri typed in the command to proceed with the anchoring process.

Within seconds large clouds of dust could be seen surrounding each of the seven construction bots. Waiting for the dust to move on, Hendrik ran some numbers to check on the available ground that the bots would use to construct the domes.

"Looking good...all the domes should be structurally sound and ready for fitting in a few days."

Extending outwards from the anchor arms, large spray nozzles aided by the low gravity, extended the fifty metres that would be the base of the habitation's foundation. The spray nozzle pressure lifting the arms as they stretched further outwards and away from the anchors. A thick grey soup started to form under the spray nozzles as the heavy liquid mixed with the Moon dust, a mixture of ground down lunar rock and solar wind deposits. Once the ground was soaked from the spray nozzle activity, each arm retracted back to the central cylinder.

"Phase two complete, starting phase three."

A large central shaft extended from the top of the construction robot's hemispherical dome. It too had five octopus-like arms that extended outwards towards the perimeter of the soon to be constructed dome. Each of the construction arms had a large angled reinforced plate the size of a bulldozer's main blade and pressurized jet nozzles to aid with the construction process.

The five heavily armoured arms had reached the dome's perimeter and now slowly started to lower into the thick grey soup, spinning around the dome as they descended.

Upon contact with the ground there was an initial creak and groan as the robot's main structure and anchor points struggled with the additional torque requirements. Then the arms with their angled blades started to raise the now hardening mass of Moon dust and construction gel upwards to start the dome's outer wall. Each construction arm's blade was angled to raise the height of the construction wall just a few degrees with each rotation. Slowly the blades would return back towards the central cylinder of the *construction-bot* as they transverse the circumference of the spiralling enclosure. Soon the outline of a dome like structure could be seen starting to form. More construction gel and Moon dust were added to the process. Occasionally the blades shuddered as they encountered some un-dissolved harder material and the process slowed slightly. More gel or pressurized hardening gas was added as required.

Eight hours later the construction robots were entombed in their own construction. Their only remaining function now was to act as the central support column and electrical power supply. Within the central shaft that supported the centre of the dome were dormant electrical generators.

"Phase three complete. Got to hand it to those engineers, that went smoothly!" said Teri, admiration in her voice.

"Starting phase four."

The initial construction phase over, the dome's interior filled with pressurised hardening gas searching for any cracks in the domes structure. Each time a leak was detected, the gas could be seen venting into the Moon's low-density atmosphere. As the gas came into contact with the lunar freezing low gravity atmosphere it hardened and formed a seal. Soon all seven domes had been made air tight.

"All domes sealed.

Starting phase five."

The remaining gas inside the domes was bombarded with tiny electrical charges making it stick to the dome's surface. The resulting gel like coating would act as a second containment wall should there be a breach of the dome's outer superstructure.

"Phase five complete," Teri turned to Hendrik giving him a thumbs up,

"Time for the next phase," she continued typing in the required commands on her console.

*

Luke, having completed his evening patrol was back in the viewing room.

"Wow! Will you take a look at that, this morning there was nothing, now seven domes. *Incredible!*"

Even Lynette was silent, quite a feat for her as she always had an opinion or smart-ass comment for just about everything.

94

"Wow Luke...Yes wow! Who would have thought man could build something like that in such a short space of time? Wait something's happening."

Seven smaller tubular shaped *bots* were speeding down the lunar surface heading for each of the seven domes.

Ten metres from the dome's shell, the *tunnel-bots* stopped. Then as one raised themselves up and onto a pivoting swing mechanism that now protruded from the base of each individual robot. A set of grinding bevel wheels thrust themselves out of the front of the raised *tunnel-bot* and started to spin. Initially the bevelled wheels started to spin slowly and then started to speed up. Soon the wheels were travelling so fast that the observers in the viewing platform could only see a singular mass of shining spinning steel. On the very outer edge of the spinning cutting wheels, laser beams that were focused ahead of the *bot* converged into a point. Then the tunnel *bot* started down into the Moon's surface. Within minutes the tunnel bots were submerged, intent on creating an access tunnel to each of the seven domes.

*

"Tunnels complete, stopping drills." reported Teri.

95

The tunnel bots had stopped three hundred millimetres short of the exterior surface of the dome.

"Right backing up," replied Hendrik.

"Dropping rear panel.

Expanding outer rear ring.

Creating seal."

A few minutes passed as the entrance access door was expanded into place.

The three-metre entry door complete, the tunnel-bots released the sealant gas into the tunnels. Soon the tunnels were sealed and the task of creating the access door into the dome could be completed.

Using its cutting lasers for more precision, the tunnel robot removed the last three hundred millimetres of rock that separated the tunnel from the dome. Then, with small careful deliberate laser guided cuts, it made the entrance to the dome. Just before the three-metre diameter door was complete, a shaft shot out of the *bot* and sank an anchor bolt into the surface of the soon to be completed door. Door secured, the final cut was made.

With a hiss and rush of escaping pressurised air, the door clanged loose. Slowly reversing back into the tunnel with its speared prize, the tunnel-bot started its crushing bevel wheels and slowly drew the hooked circular piece of dome wall towards the deadly spinning gears of destruction. Within minutes nothing remained of the access door taken from the dome's wall.

"Now for the tricky bit," Teri whispered to herself.

"Starting phase seven," stated Hendrik.

The tunnel-bot slowly edged its way forward towards the aperture, adjusting its height with small protruding feet based around its circumference. It shuffled forward like an old man hooked up to a nebulizer awaiting his next intake of breath to power the oxygen starved muscles.

Once halfway through the hole the tunnel-bot stopped. Excreting a dark gel around the hole into which it had crept, the substance started to solidify on contact with the domes surface creating a tough vacuum proof seal.

"Seal complete.

Now for phase eight."

Loud gunshot bangs could be heard as explosive bolts fired inside the robot's interior. The front of the tunnel-bot sheared off and in a clockwise rotation turned until it was hanging from the last remaining intact bolt. Inside the tunnel-bot a grappling harpoon, attached to fifty metres of folded cable linked together in a triangular pattern, moved into position protruding from the front of the machine. A laser guided targeting system made a red dot on the target plate attached to the dome's central shaft.

"Checking trajectory...

All green...

Ready to fire...

Do you want the honours Teri?" asked Hendrik.

"Absolutely!"

"In five...four...three...two...one...

Mark!"

Teri fired the harpoon.

"Bulls eye!" whispered Teri.

The triangular shaped steel rope bridge hung loosely between the harpoon and the tunnel bot.

"Time to tension the ropes,"

Hendrik typed in the command to reel in the bridge. A few minutes later the wire rope bridge was pre-stressed and no longer sagging.

"All done, now to install the walkway."

The tunnel material previously ground up and stored in the tunnel bots internal mechanisms started to creep forward along the wire bridge, hardening as it went. The progress was slow but steady. A few hours later a completed walkway hung between the habitation's central shaft and the tunnel bot.

"Right then only six more to go," Teri said without enthusiasm.

Within a week all habitation domes had an access tunnel complete with walkway to the central shaft.

*

Chris, looking out through the observation view and marvelled at how quickly those grey engineers had constructed and erected the slingshot mechanism from

MOON

the *Guardian's* blueprints. Developed in the Growth Pods, these four-armed humans had been genetically modified for work in space. A thick outer poly-organic skin, similar to that of the green enforcers, protected them from the cold of space and the sun's radiation. Enabled with gecko like sticky filaments on the base of their feet, they never needed to be attached to the defence ring's surface. A nice touch even if he did say so himself.

The only limitation of these grown engineers was their need to replenish their resources and breathe an oxygenated atmosphere. Resyk paste had to flown up from the planet Resyk centres and used to replenish these valuable commodities. The breather masks used small vials of water which broke down into its base gases for the user to consume. Also a flown in expensive resource, but without them the grey engineers that were so efficient would be useless.

"All very efficient but time consuming," *Chris* said to no one in particular.

A portion of the docking bay had to be turned into a mess hall and bunk room. Being human, although modified, they still required a small amount of rest, four hours sleep seemed to be the optimum amount needed. Then half an hour three times a day for restocking their food pouches.

100

Once the slingshot was constructed and the engineers returned to the vats for Resyk, the docking bays would be used to transfer the transport modules to the slingshot area. From there they could be sent to the catchment funnel on the Moon.

Leaving the slingshot viewing room, *Chris* walked along the brightly lit white corridor to the energy catchment section. Here he surveyed the catchment funnel construction recently started by the assigned engineering staff. A fifty-metre diameter fan like structure was beginning to take shape. When complete it could be used to catch the energy balls created in the new power plant on the Moon. Once created in the Moon's magnetic shield chambers, the energy balls would be encased in a shield and fired towards the catchment funnel here or on Earth. If sent here the casing would be removed and inserted into the existing energy generator before being beamed down to the receiving station on Earth. Plan "A" was to fire the energy balls directly to earth, but as he knew, always have a plan "B".

There would be some downtime when the changeover from the existing beaming in technology, to the new energy ball generation technology was implemented. *Chris* made a mental note to grow a thousand *green enforcers* in each city just in case the

101

people got restless and reverted back to their more primitive instincts.

He was pleased with the progress that the Moon construction team had reported. So far all was on schedule. He was right to put Hendrik and Teri together as a team. They were both narcissistic, but in each other's presence seemed to respect the others point of view as they were both perfectionists. Strange bedfellows, but there you are!

Down on Earth the habitation modules were nearing completion. The guilds seemed to be cooperating extremely efficiently. He would have used them for the modifications and construction work on the defence ring, but the *Guardians* had insisted on implementing a policy of no naturally born human was to be involved in the construction or maintenance of the defence ring. As they were known to have access to the prediction machine back on *Termite*, *Chris* deemed it prudent to continue with the same policy.

Council members and initiates of the eighteenth order were ferried up and down as required. The only exception to these rules lay with the privileged seven members of his inner circle. They could come and go as they pleased.

Nearly all of the ring's processes and mechanisms were automated. For the few that required a hands-on approach, operation technicians had been grown and were attached to their stations ready to intervene should any action be required. Being fed via an umbilical cord attached directly to their food pouches, just enough energy was supplied to them to maintain their health and awareness. The Resyk facility on the defence ring rarely required maintenance.

Chris, looking down at his liver spotted hands, started to scratch a particularly dry patch of skin.

"Where is that *ATS*?

I feel that I am getting weaker and weaker, I need to be regenerated," he vocalised, concern in his voice.

Turning back into the corridor, *Chris* strode towards the docking bay.

*

XHOSETI

MOON

ASTEROID

BELT

MOON

Chapter Seven

Space

Asteroid Belt

24 Million miles from Earth

The loosely formed spearhead of the *ATS* formation seemed to be drifting and pulling apart. Every few minutes a small red beacon would flash on the northern *ATS* formation only to be greeted in response by the southern *ATS* formation with blue retaliatory flashing.

In the centre of the overlapping spearheads remained the dark vacuum of something immense. Nothing stirred in that dark void; even the occasional asteroid intent on passing through the apparent aperture seemed to avoid that part of space.

Slowly, the two *ATS* asteroids at the head of their respective arrows, started to move slightly further away from the formation. Both had moved well enough away from the formation to now appear to be breaking away.

Just as they were both far enough away from the main group of *ATS's* to cloak and head off to their respective self-appointed assignments, there appeared to be a disturbance in the central void where the formations overlapped each other.

A gigantic golden asteroid began to de-cloak and soon shimmered into view. The *ATS's,* normally in loose formation, appeared to stand to attention, forming rigid sharp lines in each faction's spearhead like formation. The two largest *ATS's* moved as if propelled by time itself and stood rigidly to attention at the head of their respective spearheads.

Now the golden asteroid fluttered and became solid. At the same time, as if in response, each of the *ATS* entities glowed the bright red or blue of their faction's alliance.

Now the central golden coloured asteroid shone brilliantly for a few seconds then blinked out and, in its place, burned a brilliant golden,

'*G*' embossed with an equally grand '*A*'

The *Grand Architect* radiated *Power,*

"AND...*WHERE...ARE...YOU...*

TWO...GOING!"

107

ATS Nine-Seven-Four glowed a faint bluish tinge and seemed to shiver,

"To help the humans *Grand Architect*," and was silent awaiting its masters wrath.

"AND...WHERE...ARE...YOU...

GOING...NUMBER...

SEVEN-SEVEN-SEVEN?"

ATS Seven-Seven-Seven glowed a dull red,

"If *Nine-Seven-Four* is going to help the humans then balance must be maintained. *Seven-Seven-Seven* will help the *Xhoseti...Grand Architect*."

The golden *'G'* and *'A'* shimmered and *blinked* out, returning the bright golden coloured asteroid which pulsated and bristled with what might be interpreted as deep intense thought.

Long agonising minutes passed as the *Grand Architect* pondered what to do with these upstart creations of theirs.

MOON

There was a *shimmer* and the golden asteroid was replaced yet again by the bright golden *'G'* and *'A'*.

"WE...HAVE...CONSULTED...WITH...

OURSELVES...AND...AGREE...

BALANCE...MUST...BE...MAINTAINED...

BOTH...SHALL...BE...REPLENISHED."

Then the *Grand Architect* shimmered again and then disappeared leaving the *ATS* spearheads yet again with the dark void of space where the golden asteroid once resided.

In the centre of the spearhead formation, where the red and blue bodies overlapped each other, appeared two golden balls one tinged blue the other red.

ATS Seven-Seven-Seven burst into action and sped into the red tinged golden ball. Extending its proboscis like arm the ball vanished into the *ATS*. There was a red flash and the *ATS* seemed to pulse and radiate with the newly acquired energy it had just consumed. A few seconds later *Seven-Seven-Seven* turned its attention to *Nine-Seven-Four*.

109

ATS *Nine-Seven-Four* sped towards the reward offered by the *Grand Architect* and almost made it to that life-giving source of energy when the red ball of energy hit it.

Shrieking in agony the rear of the attacked *ATS* started to melt and tear away. Now weak with lack of energy, the crippled *ATS* feebly sent up a shield with its last remaining ounces of energy drawing deeply on what was left of its rapidly dwindling reserves.

RED closed in savouring the moment, took a gloating few seconds to gather its energy for a final end to its adversary when both *ATS* were engulfed in a bright ball of golden light,

"DESIST...RED...

THERE...MUST...BE...BALANCE!"

Held in the grip of the golden grasp of the *Grand Architect*, *Seven-Seven-Seven* struggled to wriggle out of the all-encompassing, golden grip. Changing shape, first a small, then a large asteroid, then cloaking and de-cloaking in a rapid flickering motion, all to no avail. Realising the futility of its attempts to escape the golden grip, *Seven-Seven-Seven* went limp.

An intense pulse of golden light wafted over *Nine-Seven-Four* and all the wounds inflicted upon it by *RED* vanished. Repaired but still weak, *Nine-Seven-Four* lay still, encompassed in the golden grip knowing that *RED* would try to kill *BLUE* again as soon as they were released.

As if with a mind of its own, the golden blue tinged ball of energy floated close to *BLUE's* bow.

Slowly, cautiously *Nine-Seven-Four* stretched out its proboscis and swallowed the glowing ball of energy.

The transformation was almost instantaneous. *BLUE* glowed with bright blue light and seemed to expand visibly.

"REMEMBER...THERE...MUST...

BE...BALANCE."

Then the golden grip was gone. *RED* turned to *BLUE,* emitted a dark red burst of light then *shimmered* and vanished.

The *ATS* spearhead formation of Reds and Blues silently went back to their loose formation, slowly drifting apart but always returning. Small rocks bounced off the apparently inert asteroid like structures once more.

111

MOON

All was quiet, all was peaceful, and all was again...

In balance...

*

"Hey Darren, what do you think of that one? Scanners show that this asteroid is full of frozen water...Out," said Sean into the grapple ship's communication mike.

"That's ice to you. Looks good but get down onto it and take a core sample. We need it to be as pure as possible, no alien bugs this time. You know the drill. Out," replied Darren.

"Yes boss," came the sarcastic reply.

"Taking her down,"

Sean fired his thrusters aiming the grapple ship towards the identified victim. The asteroid loomed larger and larger in his cockpits screen.

"Man this is a big one!"

"That's not what the girls back home tell me," retorted Darren.

112

"Is that you or me they're talking about skipper?" countered Sean.

"Keep the chatter to a minimum Sean. *Out!*"

Closing in on the asteroid as big as a large space cruiser, Sean made a sweep around the asteroid to gauge its size.

"Looks like its eight hundred and seventy-six metres long with an average girth of three hundred and sixty-five metres. Out.

Proceeding to targeted anchor position."

Selecting what looked like a suitable flat landing area, Sean pushed the harpoon button on his dash board. A target screen appeared on his view finder. The grapple ship's thrusters automatically pitched and rolled the small craft to align with the rotation of the asteroid.

On the screen the crosshairs lined up with each other and a green light flashed in his helmet visor.

"Firing. Out."

There was a faint recoil as the harpoon's jets fired and sent the projectile towards its intended target.

113

"Yeah, bulls eye. He shoots, he scores…and the crowd goes wild. Sorry boss. Out."

Reeling in the harpoon's cable, the grapple craft slowly pulled itself down to the surface of the asteroid.

There was a loud clunk as the grappler drawn ship impacted the rocky surface.

"All down, a bit bumpy, but all systems check green. Good to go for core sample. Out."

"Good work Sean, nice one. Now let's get a sample of this *frozen water*. Out."

A flap opened towards the stern of the craft and a small round tube pushed its way out of the little scout ship's exterior. Attached to the tube was a sphere with a red glowing tip. The tip started to glow red hot as the laser shot out of the sphere's tip and started melting the frozen surface below it.

A few minutes later the laser shut off and the sphere rotated forty-five degrees exposing another tubular like extremity. Extending the tube down into the precision cut shaft the tube started to vibrate as it travelled down into the exposed ice.

114

"Got the core sample...Testing for contamination. Out. "

Soon a printout appeared on Sean's console.

"*Jackpot!*

Looks like we struck gold, the readings indicate no foreign bodies in the water...Crystal clear pure unadulterated hydrogen and two atoms of oxygen. Out."

"Yes, very good, not bad for a third attempt. Good job too as we don't have enough fuel to get us back to base," said Darren out loud forgetting the microphone was still engaged.

"What? When were you going to share that piece of critical life changing information with me?" exclaimed Sean.

"Need to know basis. You did not need to know and still don't. Slip of the tongue so to speak. Don't worry about it, it did not happen so no foul, *no harm. Out!*"

Back on the grappler's mother-ship, Darren stared at the console in front of him. He gave the fuel tank gauge another tap with his finger. The gauge rose a little to indicate more fuel than he knew was really there. He

115

MOON

waited a few seconds and then watched the fuel level indicator drop back down into the red.

"Set your alignment beacon, I'm coming to your location. Proceed with full anchor point connection. Out."

On the grapple scout ship Sean typed in the command to extend the anchor arms. Slowly the arms extended, tips holding the explosive charges that would fire the five-pronged spikes down into the surface of the asteroid.

"Arms extended. All green...Firing."

There was a shudder and jerk as the harpoon counteracted the effects of the charges by reeling in the cable to make it as taut as possible without over tensioning the wire rope.

Checking the anchor bolts embedment strength, the screen flashed numbers in front of Sean's viewer.

"Anchors look good. All green. You are clear to attach mother to baby. Out."

Setting the mother-ship to auto pilot, Darren leaned back in his captain's chair and strapped himself in with the restraint belts. This was always the least favourite part of any operation for Darren. Giving complete control over to

116

any type of robot always made him feel redundant, even helpless.

The mother-ship fired its thrusters and propelled itself towards the homing beacon. Red lights flashed on the fuel panels.

"DANGER...Low Fuel...

DANGER...Low Fuel...

DANGER...Low Fuel...

Time to fuel depletion in...

Ten seconds...

Nine seconds...

Eight seconds...

Seven seconds..."

The mother-ship moved into place aligning itself with the asteroids rotation.

"Six seconds..."

Thrusters fired sending the larger vessel down towards the scout ship now firmly fixed to the surface of the asteroid.

117

MOON

"Five seconds..."

"Just a few more metres to go," said Darren between clenched teeth.

"Four seconds..."

With a clunk and hiss the mother-ship docked with the smaller scout ship.

"Three seconds of fuel remain...

RECOMMEND REFUEL AS PRIORITY ONE...

RECOMMEND REFUEL AS PRIORITY ONE...

RECOMMEND REFUEL AS PRIORITY ONE..."

The screen flashed its warning in bright red letters.

Cancelling the warning, Darren typed in a new command.

"Checking seal with scout ship,"

A whirring mechanical noise emanated from the air lock at the base of the craft.

MOON

"All green, lock is tight. I repeat. Lock is tight. Welcome back Sean. See you in meeting room one in five. Out."

*

"Now that we have latched onto the asteroid it's time to refill the tanks before we can head back to the Moon and land this monster," began Darren as soon as Sean sat down.

"What I need you to do is tell me how long it's going to take to melt down what we need so I can fire up the stabilising thrusters and then get us back on course," continued Darren.

Sean leaning back in his chair lifted his legs and plonked them confrontationally down on the meeting room's small table.

"Sure thing boss, but first we need to discuss this lack of communication between us and you nearly jeopardising all the work we have done out here. Not to mention the disappointment you would have brought to all those female drain on resources I have back at base when they find my desiccated husk of a corpse," said Sean confrontationally staring Darren directly in the eyes.

119

MOON

"Umm, well...ok then," started Darren, "what's it going to take for you to completely forget about this near miss?"

A smile formed on Sean's lips, "*Nothing!* I just wanted you to admit that you fucked up and now I have it all recorded," Sean pulled the voice recorder from his top pocket and waved it in the air.

"So, finally the true face of deception shows itself. Well I'll not bite; do what you want with it. Now back to business and get your boots of my meeting room table!"

Darren continued going through the check list he had been prepared a few minutes before Sean had entered the room.

With a bit of a swagger, Sean left the meeting room softly whistling to himself.

*

A few hours later when enough ice had been vaporised for the refuel, the mother-ship was ready to begin the stabilisation process.

"Time to commence stabilisation...Ten seconds and counting,"

MOON

Both Sean and Darren were sitting in the control centre staring up at the continuously revolving mass of rocks above them.

"Three seconds to burn..." came the silky female sounding voice over the speaker system.

"Two seconds to burn...

One second to burn...

Mark...

Initiating burn..."

There was a shudder as the recently refuelled rocket thrusters kicked into life. The superstructure of the spacecraft creaked and groaned as the huge thrusters attempted to stop the rotation of the asteroid.

Slowly the rotating cylinder of frozen water spun down and eventually groaned to a halt. The ice structure, now stable and under the control of the mother-ship's thrusters started to edge its way out of the asteroid belt and on its previously prepared rendezvous with Earth's Moon.

MOON

Heading for Earth and its Moon, the asteroid slowly started picking up speed as it travelled. Within a few weeks the asteroid was nearing its destination.

Their previous cat and mouse escapades forgotten, Darren and Sean settled into the role of effective astronaut technicians; checking and rechecking all the ships systems. Nothing was left to chance; no engine failures could be afforded. Just one small error and this gigantic mobile rock would smash into the Moon destroying all that man had created there. The power generation station would be obliterated by the very thing that was to be used to keep the human occupants alive.

"Not much longer until you will be back in the loving arms of your drain on resources Sean," Darren joked to his colleague.

"Time to reverse this sucker and prepare for slingshot braking," replied Sean ignoring Darren's taunt.

Turning to his console, Sean started running through the braking procedure.

"According to the numbers, we should be approaching the dark side of the Moon in just a few more days. Let me just run the numbers again,"

MOON

A further ten silent minutes passed as the calculations were re-entered into the computer and evaluated.

"Yep, they are all correct! We need to start the braking procedure in approximately two hours. I'll start the countdown clock for reverse thrusters burn in...

Three...Two...One

Mark...

Countdown started,"

The Earth with its Moon, was getting larger and larger with every passing minute. Soon it would be time to fire up the rockets and reverse the trajectory of this gigantic cylinder of ice.

The computer's familiar silky voice emitted from the control rooms speaker system,

"Three seconds to burn...

Two seconds to burn...

One second to burn...

Mark...

MOON

Initiating Burn."

Slowly the asteroid started spinning in the opposite direction to the way it had been initially rotating. The ships thrusters automatically rotated and pivoted to control and stabilise the asteroid's trajectory.

"Looking good there!

All tanks full and burn is stable," observed Darren.

"Approaching the Moon's gravitational pull," whispered Sean, tension evident in his quiet demeanour.

A few tense minutes passed.

"Nicely done. All stable and locked into the Moon's gravitational pull," said Darren wiping a single bead of sweat from his brow.

As the asteroid travelled around the colder, shady side of the Moon, minute cracking of the asteroid's surface could be felt reverberating through the superstructure of the space craft.

"Is that normal?" said Sean turning to Darren.

"Nothing to worry about I'm sure just the ice freezing up a little as the effects of the Moon's gravity compresses the cracks in the asteroid," came the reply.

124

"Well if the asteroid is compressing on the dark side what will happen when we enter the sunlit side?" questioned Sean worriedly.

"Shit, I don't know but prepare for separation. Buckle yourself in, this could get bumpy."

As the asteroid peeked the tip of its head around the dark side of the Moon and into the now brightly sunlit part of space, violent shuddering could be felt running through the craft's frame.

Cracks started appearing on the surface of the asteroid as water defrosted and changed state from solid to liquid and then gas. The rapid change in pressure created spouting geyser like tubes of water high above the asteroid's surface, altering the asteroid's course. The asteroid started to spin, rapidly becoming uncontrollable as the mother-ship's thrusters fired and pivoted all to no avail.

"Fuck...now what?" shouted Sean to Darren.

Each time the Moon came back into focus on their view port it appeared closer and closer. Now the power generation station was in view.

"We have to detach!"

MOON

"Time to impact twenty seconds," came the emotionless voice over the speaker system.

"Do it!...JUST DO IT!" shouted Sean.

"COME ON!...GET US OUT OF HERE.

HIT THE EJECT BUTTON FOR GOD'S SAKE!"

Lifting a panel on the console, Darren slammed his hand down on the large exposed red button.

Explosive bolts fired, and the mother-ship tore away from the smaller surface bound scout ship. Thrusters firing the ship sped up and away from the now doomed asteroid.

*

Luke, having finished his first inspection walk-down of the day was looking out of the Moon generator's viewing port staring in awe at the rising majestic blue ball of life that he called home. He was just marvelling at the beautiful scene when a shaft of white gas caught his eye. Now having got his attention, Luke focused on what it could be. He soon realised that it was some sort of out of control rock and that it was heading straight for him and the rest of the generator crew.

MOON

"Lynette you have to get up here now! There's a frigging asteroid heading our way and it looks on target, reckon we have three minutes till it hits us!"

"Stop taking the piss Luke, you know that kind of thing isn't funny," came the reply.

"NO JOKES! GET UP HERE NOW!"

A minute later Lynette stood before a pointing Luke.

"Any last confessions?" Luke whispered.

The small ball of rock with its bursts of white vapour suddenly seemed to veer to the left as a larger burst of gas came from its tumbling surface. Moments later a mining ship rocketed away from the out of control mass of ice and rock.

Lynette grabbed Luke in a death gripping hug, tears streaming from her eyes,

"I don't want to die like this! Anything else, just not ripped to pieces like a rag doll because some stupid mining engineer got their calculations wrong!"

The tumbling asteroid loomed larger and larger blotting out the once beautiful view of the Earth.

MOON

Moments before impact a bright blue light appeared on the starboard side of the asteroid.

ATS Nine-Seven-Four, aware of the catastrophe that was about to unfold, shimmered and de-cloaked.

Swelling with the newly acquired power received from the *Grand Architect,* the *ATS BLUE* visibly grew tenfold in size and attached itself to the out of control extinction sized rock. With a blinding blue burst of light the *ATS* took the asteroid up and over the human constructed generator buildings.

Straining with exertion, *BLUE* flew the asteroid to the dark and cold side of the Moon, gently landing it on the surface a few hundred metres South of the now depleted ice mines.

During the construction of the first generator buildings the Moon had been scanned to check what minerals and deposits could be harvested and used as construction materials. In the very centre of the dark side of the Moon, a deposit of ice had been located. Having never been exposed to the heating effects of the sun, the asteroids laden with ice that had impacted with the Moon simply gravitated over time to this central location.

Once located, an ice mining facility was established and the processed ice, now water, was pumped to the *Resyk* centre back at the generator station. Having been mined out many years earlier, the mining station had been abandoned and moth-balled. The pipes were empty, the buildings dead and eerily silent, no lights shone in the viewing ports it was now just a defunct shell. The mine might as well have been the remnants of a long lost, ancient alien outpost. Soon though, the mine would have to be re-activated and brought back in to service thanks to the actions of *BLUE*.

Having averted the destruction of the generator station and all of its inhabitants the *ATS* cloaked again and sped off to Earth's defence ring searching for its cohabitation human, the now *Grand Master*.

Within moments the cloaked *ATS* had entered the space dock.

*

Chris, suddenly drawn to the docking bay stopped reviewing the reports that had been piling up in his Inbox, put down his review rod and stepped out of his office. Not knowing why or even exactly where he was going, he found himself in docking bay one. It was then that *BLUE*

129

pounced; extending its oesophagus like arm, it swept up *Chris* and swallowed him into the depths of the *ATS.*

"Aaah...I had wondered when you would return," projected *Chris* to the biomechanical entity.

A series of images flashed through *Chris's* mind, the *RED ATS* firing and almost killing *BLUE,* the *Grand Architect* saving *BLUE* and then the replenishing effect the golden ball of energy had had on the *ATS.* The fiasco with the asteroid and its crew. The towing of the ice laden rock ending with it being gently placed outside the mining facility, so the humans could mine it.

"Thank you my friend, thank you for everything you have done for us yet again. I have been eagerly awaiting your return as I too am in need of your aid. As you can see my body is failing. Is there anything you can do for me?"

There was a short pause and then *Chris* blacked out.

Bones started dissolving, tearing and ripping of muscles from those soon to be dissolved bones, made soft slippery squelching sounds as they were stretched and formed into newer longer and stronger ones. No human could take the deconstruction process alive. *Chris's* mind slept on, enjoying some peaceful memories of his mother

MOON

back in Ireland before his fourth birthday, before he had become the man that he was a few minutes ago.

Soon the bones were being re-knitted and enhanced with more iron and calcium than his fellow human beings. With stronger bone comes the need for bigger and stronger muscles and organs. Soon the process of replacing the organs and reattaching the muscles was at an end.

The *ATS* flew down to *Guardian City* and landed in *Chris's* quarters waiting for the regeneration process to be completed.

*

131

MOON

XHOSETI

MOON

EARTH

PREFAB

MODULES

MOON

Chapter Eight

Earth

City One - Guardian

Fabrication Plant

Landing the *ATS* in front of the assembly plant, *Chris* mentally projected,

"*Expel*"

Standing in front of the impressive *Plasti-Granite* building *Chris* inspected his appearance in the dark mirror like reflection of the smooth unblemished wall before him. What a fine job *BLUE* had done. The white hair and beard had vanished, in its place shone a shiny bald and smooth faced young man of approximately twenty-five human years of age. The eyes were the same though, grey and piercing with a slight touch of silver, a side effect of the *Morph-Suit*.

He felt taller, stronger and young again, just as he had the first time he had exited the *ATS* over two thousand seven hundred years ago.

"Thank you again my friend," he projected to the *ATS* which glowed slightly, shimmered and then vanished.

An opening appeared in the building where *Chris* was admiring his new appearance.

"Welcome back *Grand Master Chris*, we have been expecting you to come visit the factory for some time now. All is proceeding well; the modules are on schedule and the new materials of construction are wonderful. We poured this...what did you call it? *Plasti-Aloid* as per your instruction. *Pumice, Plasti-Oil, Tantalum* for ductility, all in the exact quantities as per your specification sheet. It is amazing!

Even at four thousand degrees it remains as tough as it is at room temperature, even in the most extreme environments. In the vacuum of space, at minus two hundred and seventy degrees Celsius, it is just as ductile and tough as if it were at ambient temperature. Truly...truly, amazing!" chattered the construction manager excitedly.

Duncan was a portly man, five-foot six inches with a friendly demeanour. His jowly face shook every time he opened his mouth to express his opinions or instructions.

135

MOON

Known for his work hard, play hard attitude when motivating his staff, Duncan was normally the first to the feast and the last to leave the table, but only after the required item of action had been completed successfully.

"Let me take you through the fabrication process. Firstly, our design engineers came up with a layout that is slightly smaller in diameter than that of the access tunnels...as per your instruction. The modules will lock together in an upright position with those requiring less gravitation effects placed on the outskirts of the Moon domes, so the work force can sleep in an upright position. The sanitation facilities will be closest to the spinning power generators, for obvious reasons. Shit don't flow uphill!" Duncan snorted at his own little joke.

Chris stared at Duncan without any sign of understanding the reference.

Turning a bright shade of pink, Duncan continued,

"Then we designed the mess hall modules, also to be placed as close to the generator central shaft as possible. The trash, which hopefully will be minimal, will then be compacted and sent to the facilities main *Resyk* processing unit. What little recycled organic matter is processed will be used as a substitute when fresh produce

136

is not available. Not my kind of fine dining!" Duncan chuckled, jowls wobbling.

"Continue," instructed *Chris.*

"So once the habitation modularised cylinders have been linked together in their respective order, we then come to the construction and assembly warehouses. This in itself makes for a challenge. You see...the size of the modules are just too small to make for any meaningful assembly area. So, my ingenious engineers came up with a rather unique method of solving this issue. Each cylinder will be capable of being split down the longitudinal axis dividing it into two parts...These assembly modules, six per dome will then be sealed together in a round circle creating an assembly area of over ten metres in diameter. The twelve external lobes, a bit like the teeth on a gear or the petals on a sunflower, can be used as machine shops for fabrication or as lay down areas for storage. The floor and ceiling will, unfortunately, need to be fabricated from locally sourced materials.

I do not see a way around that issue.

I suppose we could ferry up plate from Earth but that should only be a last option. A bottom loading iris must be fabricated to allow for the ingress of assembly

137

MOON

materials and an exit one for the removal of the final assembled piece of equipment."

"Sounds like you have thought it all through Duncan. Very impressive, now take me to the module assembly area."

Duncan lead *Chris* through the offices of the fabrication plant and out into the workshop area.

"Here we are in the initial shell moulding area. Firstly, a mould had to be made for each different type of module. The habitation cylinders were first to be extruded; a few teething problems getting the thickness and extrusion timing right, but we got there in the end. The biggest issue was how to attach the propellant tanks and the rockets. In the end we ended up adding integral ancillary attachment points. Two stage extrusion moulding just did not appear feasible. There was the need to remove the excess water in the tanks and the rockets themselves before the modules will fit through the catchment funnels aperture. So they will be attached manually and removed with explosive bolts when up on the Moon. The catchment funnel has been redesigned to have the correct size slots to enable their removal once modular ingress down the funnel's aperture is initiated," explained Duncan.

Taking a deep breath and slowly exhaling, the construction manager continued,

"As the cylinders are to be fitted together and interlocked, no method of access can be manufactured without compromising the strength of the outer casing. So, all interior components had to be prefabricated using the *Plasti-Carbonate* printer.

The internal sleeping quarters proved to be the least challenging; the anchor locations were embedded into the shell during the extrusion process and prefabricated furniture lowered into place and melded to the attachment points before the shell could harden. That being said, we are still having teething problems with the sanitation modules.

Rest assured though, I have my best team on it. I am told that a better, safer and more robust process is due to be trialled next week."

"Yet again Duncan all very impressive! Please express my amazement and gratitude to your teams. I am still unsure how the modules will be finished and then installed though. So please continue."

"Now here's the issue. When the extrusion process is complete there is no ingress to the inner working of the

139

cylinders. All power, electronic controls and guidance systems will need to be attached to the exterior of the module. This in turn will create resistance during flight. I am sure our programmers will be able to compensate for it though. That is, after they have adjusted for the effect of the Ferris wheel sling shot that we are proposing to use in propelling the modules into the atmosphere. They will be powered by the same generators used on the first Moon power station. Their gravitational pull will be used to rotate the sling shot."

"Well it sounds like you have it all under control Duncan. The right man for the right job so to speak. Is there anything else I should be aware of?" asked *Chris*.

"There is one more thing. When the sealed units are bolted together in the dome, an aperture will need to be cut through some of the cylinders to allow access through them. We are sending up a *Cut-Bot* to aid with this process. It will come complete with chemical plasma cutters as none of the normal cutting instruments will be able to get through the new *Plasti-Aloid* shell.

"Not as simple as some believe then?" offered Chris.

"No *Grand Master*, not at all. Still we are on target but may slip a little should some unforeseeable and irresolvable issue arise."

MOON

"Good man, thank you for the explanations and the tour, but I must get back to my other official duties. Please be so kind as to escort me back to the entrance,"

Both men headed back to the office block.

*

Soon *Chris* was back in the *ATS* and moments later arrived at his lodgings on the upper deck of the central habitation tube.

"Expel" he projected to *BLUE*.

Standing in his courtyard *Chris* immediately felt the presence of the *seven*.

"Show yourselves!" Chris projected.

As one the *seven*-materialised bowing to their master.

"Reports!"

One by one the *seven* went through their monthly reports of the happenings of each city.

A few minor uprisings amongst the dissatisfied anti-establishment groups. Nothing that the *seven* could not resolve quickly and quietly.

141

MOON

"Good. I will rely on your judgement as to when the *Enforcers* will be required so keep a careful eye on the anti-establishment leaders. We must know when they are going to incite unrest. I suspect it will be during the power outage during the change-over period."

Callum, stepping forward, cleared his throat, "Master...there is one that would not be dissuaded from her path of chaos. A fiery redheaded monster of a woman from City Three named Greta. She claims that the *Guardians* caused the last War, so they could subjugate all the survivors and rule as the kings of the Middle Ages of old Earth.

We know this to be partially true but with good cause. If they had not initiated the *Third World War* the *Xhoseti* would have been triumphant and mankind destroyed or worse...harvested. I have entered her dreams and shown her this possible outcome of events, but she is too strong willed and determined to expose the truth to all who will listen. Already there are hundreds who take her word over the *Guardians.* She cannot be reasoned with, I'm afraid that there may not be any alternative but to silence her, *for good!*"

"No Callum, I am sure it will not come to that. Besides, if she has such a following then there is the

142

possibility of her becoming a martyr. That can only make things worse!

No, you are to keep an eye on her and let us hope that her sermons only amount to rumour. If we play this right she will discredit herself given time.

Keep calm and keep me informed."

Callum nodded his approval and returned to the circle awaiting more instruction.

"Soon we will need to help with the administration of the power station up on the Moon. Well, administration may be the wrong word, more like peace keeping. I am sure there will be many an ego that gets ruffled and if there is any tension, quell it before it spreads.

This anti-establishment woman Greta, will try to use the frustration and conflict to incite unrest. She may even recruit agents to initiate tension. We must find those undercover agents and remove them from the project. That task I will leave to the seven of you.

Now it is time for me to attend to the whims of the council. Let us convene again prior to the first module launch unless something urgent arises," finished *Chris*.

143

MOON

The *seven* bowed and as one cloaked, leaving *Chris* to his thoughts.

In the corridor just outside the penthouse, Willow sort out Khanya through a mind link.

"Are you there Khanya?"

"Yes Willow, what is it?"

"I believe we should investigate this Greta, something just does not add up. No one would willingly want the Xhoseti to have won. No matter what the price! Do you concur?"

"I do, but stealth is the key here. If Callum gets wind of what we are up too he will be offended. Not something I would want. He seems to never reveal his capabilities, always holding back. I wonder what his true agenda is?"

"Good, discretion at all costs. I will meet you in the nine hundred metre market tomorrow," replied Willow through the mind link.

Still cloaked, both Khanya and Willow made their way to the travel shaft and left the central habitation tube.

At the far end of the corridor the light seemed to shimmer and distort.

MOON

De-cloaking Callum pondered the conversation he had just overheard. They were right though, he did not reveal his true potential. Picking up on their thoughts was a skill he had mastered a long time ago with the aid of his beloved Greta. The mere thought of her sent a shiver of pleasure down his spine, how he missed her.

Was he enthralled, bewitched? Words could not explain the hold she had on him. She knew the truth about the *Guardians* and their role in the demise of the last world order. Where she had got that information from he had no idea, it must have been her incredible talent to read minds. Something she had used to influence people for that additional basket of fruit or to get an item of clothing she just had to have. Had she used her abilities on him to make him feel the way he did? Callum did not care, she just made sense, she made him feel...*complete*.

The *Guardians* should be held accountable for what they had done to the human race. Every time he was away from her he felt a longing in his chest, almost a pain. It felt like a cramp deep down in his torso, something he always hid from the *Grand Master* when in his presence.

It was time to return to her and breathe in her calming effect.

MOON

Bewitched, Callum strode towards the travel shaft intent on returning to City Three with a sense of urgency, so he could be back in her presence...back with the centre of his universe.

*

Chris, sitting in one of the few items of furniture in the room, went over the progress so far. His presentation to the council members would have to impress all of them, but especially the political sect. Vice chairman Jeremy would be rooting for the project to fail so he could initialize a motion for hydrocarbon power generation; something *Chris* would stop at all costs. They were not going to start that gigantic ball rolling again. Once in motion, the need for cheap and easily obtainable fossil fuels would spiral out of control again, just as it had in the twentieth century.

Chris rose from the comfortable arm chair he was sitting in. Something was bothering him. He could not quite put his finger on it. Something about Callum's demeanour, he seemed to offer only the problem, not the solution. Allowing this redhead to spread her words of dissent could only lead to trouble.

"I need to find out more about this woman Greta," *Chris* said out loud to the empty room.

146

Returning to his armchair *Chris* continued to prepare his presentation.

*

XHOSETJ

MOON

XHOSETI

MOON

,

149

Chapter 9

Moon

Tunnels

Xhespo lay in wait, watching the white grotesque rats huddle together for warmth. Careful not to get close to the red fungus, she made herself as quiet as possible. Her shell was dark in nature with a few streaks of white where the Moon dust had collected and formed small striations. The small meal each of these tiny rodents provided only served to keep her alive...not thrive; she must find a larger more sustainable source of nutrition. On occasion she had seen one of those hated humans walk around in the generator hall. If there was only one of them then that would not be sustainable either. The rats appeared to be settling down for their evening slumber. The red fungus was now the hunted; each time the air bubble expanded with the escaping gas from the human's airlock, it encroached on the red fungus's territory.

A rat would dart out holding its breath and the fungus would attach itself to the rodent covering it almost completely. Then the rodent would run back to the air pocket and the fungus would flare bright red and end up

150

as a thick sticky nutritious gel which the rats would tear into.

Xhespo stretched out a claw and in a quick sweeping motion snatched the unsuspecting rodent from its huddled group of safety. *Xhespo*, no longer content with waiting for the rodent to asphyxiate, despatched the rodent's life with a quick squeeze of the claw before the mammal could release its cry for help. The rest of the pack shuddered together as if all were having the same nightmare. Prize in claw, *Xhespo* scuttled back down the wall of the generator hall and into the tunnels.

Resting in one of the tunnels after dissolving her latest source of nutrition, *Xhespo* knew that she needed to explore the rest of the shafts she had discovered. The risk of encountering the red fungus lingered in her mind, but this frivolous existence would not ensure the continuation of the *Xhoseti*...something more needed to be done. New resources needed to be found! Humans would be the best source of nutrition for her and her offspring.

Travelling down the first shaft she came to, she reached the bottom where it continued in a long-curved bend. It was as if she was walking inside a pipe of some sort. Cautiously at first, then with growing confidence, *Xhespo* continued down the pipe. Within an hour of seemingly pointless exertion, she came to a break in the pipe where the Moon dust had cut clean through its exterior surface. The subsequent movement of the dust had eroded away a large portion of the man-made pipe.

Cautiously sticking her mandibles out of the gap, she tested this new environment. Cold...stale... no sign of resources.

Exiting the pipe, *Xhespo* found herself in a large cavern filled with what could only be mining machinery. Searching her mind, she remembered encountering similar types of human machinery on *Termite* when they had overrun the human defence systems. How she remembered gorging herself on those soft juicy humans. The small ones were the most succulent. Her mandibles dribbled digestive juices on the floor making a slight hissing noise as it made contact with the man-made structure.

Now where were her warriors, where were her hatchlings? Dead...All were dead. Those hated humans will pay, but first time to explore.

Standing upright on her rear four legs *Xhespo* took stock of her surroundings. Covered generators...covered heaters...covered crushing machines. Tanks, pumps, all covered and inert. Pipes led to and from the tanks and pumps. In the far corner a man-sized door hung ajar.

Heading straight for the open door, *Xhespo* tested the atmosphere again for any signs of resources. Nothing...

Continuing down the corridor, various closed and apparently locked doors flashed past as she made her way rapidly towards the object that had caught her attention. Another open door held motionlessly open by some unseen force. Making her way through the open door she came to the observation room. It was then that a bright blue light in the sky caught her attention. A small shiny cylinder was apparently in control of a large rock with shafts of frozen white columns sticking out of it. To her amazement the shiny cylinder lowered the gigantic rock and gently set it down on the Moon's surface a few hundred metres away from the view port. Then, without a sound, it shimmered and vanished leaving the dead rock to settle.

Staying absolutely still until she was certain the blue cylinder had disappeared, *Xhespo* turned her gaze around the room. Human sitting benches lay scattered around the room, some upright, some overturned. A few even had their legs broken; it was as if a minor skirmish had taken place. Not concerned with the viewing room she went toward the only other open doorway in the room. Stretching her mandibles around the edge of the opening

153

she strained for any source of nutrition. Small faint chemical odours wafted her way, dried and desiccated odours. Hurriedly she scampered into the new room. There, up against the wall, were ten cages full of desiccated and dried out rodents. One of the cage doors was ajar. That must explain the rats in the generator room. They came from this building and when the airlock seals broke, only those that escaped down the pipes to the generator room must have survived.

Nutrition for the immediate future had been found.

Continuing through the room filled with beakers, microscopes and shiny tables, she made her way to the next room. This room was filled with basins and toilets; the human stench of defecation still hung in the oxygen depleted atmosphere.

Moving on, she came to the room that she was looking for. What did the humans call it?

"A feeding hall."

Finding a table with two rings on it, *Xhespo* pressed down on the pressure plate. With a hiss and a small pop, a dark round ball of protein appeared on the disk-shaped plate.

MOON

Sinking her proboscis into the gelatinous like substance, *Xhespo* sucked up the contents.

Pressing on the adjacent plate, a light bluish coloured liquid filled ball appeared. Sucking up the balls contents, *Xhespo* felt the vitamin enriched fluid fill her internal sacs, swelling them until she felt an almost forgotten bulging feeling. Satisfied, she turned to inspect the rest of the room. Bright silver tables and chairs littered the room. Laid out in an orderly block-like formation, every chair and table appeared to have purpose. The bright white walls terminated at both ceiling and floor with a curved smooth finish ensuring no corner could unwittingly be turned into a trap for bacteria or dirt. The sterility of the mess hall ensured that the users of this room were here for one purpose and one purpose only; to replenish their depleted energy stores and rehydrate their bodies.

As she turned around, there was a shimmer at the far end of the mess hall and *ATS Seven-Seven-Seven* blinked into reality.

Startled, *Xhespo* crouched behind the table she had just fed at. Cautiously *Xhespo* tested the air with her mandibles again. No threat emanated from the strange silver tube that appeared to be waiting silently. The silver tube had a faint red tinge to it and emblazoned on the side facing her were three sevens offset at one hundred and twenty degrees from each other. Each of the sevens strangely resembled a human leg terminating in a foot. *Xhespo* drew the comparison from the many human legs she had severed and dissolved after the invasion of *Termite.*

Then the radiating tube turned and slowly made its way out of the mess hall, retracing *Xhespo's* steps. It paused as if waiting for her to follow, then continued slowly back down through the research room and into the corridor until back in the industrial hanger.

Darting from corner to corner of each of the rooms, *Xhespo* followed *RED.*

The *ATS* went to the end of the building and paused, waiting to ensure that *Xhespo* had followed.

Projecting a laser cutting probe, *RED* began burning a hole through the dome of the mining facility. Soon a precision cut hole the size of the *ATS* appeared, and the *ATS* inched its way forward, forming a neat and perfectly cut tunnel.

Xhespo watched with interest as the new, apparently friendly, entity created this tunnel which she was sure was for her benefit.

As the rear end of the tunnelling machine slipped into the tunnel...it paused, seemed to vibrate and shimmer, then a veil came down to conceal the entrance to the shaft and it was gone.

Xhespo, now curious but still cautious, waited and watched the area where she knew the entrance to the tunnel was. Nothing...no movement, all was still. Eventually curiosity got the better of her and she crept up to the concealed entrance. Extending her mandibles, she tested for the tunnel creator.

Nothing!

Waiting again, not knowing what to do, she felt a presence in her mind, filling it with visions of tasty humans at the end of the tunnel. Her mandibles dripped in anticipation. The urge to get to and devour those hated humans was too much for her to bear; leaning against the structure she poked her claw into the wall. The texture seemed soft, almost gel like, very similar to the protein ball in the mess hall.

Pushing her claw further into the doorway, she experienced a blurring change in her surrounding and was sucked through the gate.

157

MOON

Standing inside the recently created tunnel, *Xhespo* marvelled at how quickly it had been formed. When her crew were digging their way through the Moon's bedrock and dust, the progress was extremely slow. To create a tunnel this long would have taken them weeks, not hours, to dig.

Extending out her right folded front arm, she touched the tunnel's surface with her claw. The walls were smooth to the touch and every three metres a reinforcement ring rimmed the diameter of the tunnel. Following the tunnel for what appeared to be an eternity; *Xhespo* eventually caught up with *RED* and could see it creating another veiled doorway into the exterior of another dome structure. Once the access gateway had been completed, the *ATS* moved backwards into the tunnel a few metres and paused.

Rotating the head of the *ATS* horizontally, *RED* started burning a new hillside hole into the wall of the tunnel. Soon a second tunnel ran away from the first, arcing in what appeared to be a circular design. At consistent intervals the *ATS* would stop, rotate the front portion of its cylindrical shell and create another hillside shaft which terminated at another dome's surface. The veiled access way soon followed. This process continued until the donut shaped tunnel system linked all seven habitation domes together.

Turning to ensure that *Xhespo* had understood the intent of the access gates and the tunnel system, the *ATS* turned into the wall of the tunnel and bore another shaft horizontally back towards the mining facility. After twenty metres of tunnelling, *RED* veered up at an angle and continued to the surface of the Moon. Exiting the tunnel and out onto the lunar surface, *RED* emerged behind a clump of boulders, effectively hiding the surface entrance to the *Xhoseti* tunnels from any but the most determined searcher.

Cloaking...*RED* shimmered and disappeared, leaving *Xhespo* to wonder at who her new ally was but silently thanking the strange craft for her chance to inflict revenge on the soon to be populated human habitation domes.

*

Greta, luxuriating on her newly acquired lounger, breathed a slight of contentment. Surveying the view from her penthouse apartment she sighed again, which was accompanied by a broad, perfectly white set of teeth, now exposed from under her dark red plump lips. The smile crossed her powdered cheeks, making her large, but perfectly formed nose hook down slightly. The smile

159

made her appear more demonic than angel as it highlighted her arched, stencilled red eyebrows.

Reaching for another nutty chocolate, she admired her perfectly manicured dark red finger nails before popping the little ball of heaven into her mouth. Sucking the chocolate slowly, she reminisced on how she had gotten here after having had such a poor start in life.

She had been born in the outskirt habitation dome of City Three where only the very poorest of the chosen scratched out a living selling their stolen wares or anything for that matter...even their bodies. Sometimes other people's bodies or parts thereof! She had learnt at an early age that god helps those who help themselves; just don't commit the thirteenth commandment:

"THOU SHALL NOT GET CAUGHT!"

Ooh, there had been many an occasion where it had been close, but luckily, who could refuse a beautiful redhead offering to please the soon to be corrupted bounty hunter with the pleasures of her body.

Then one day, whilst walking down an alleyway, in a shady part of the city, the miracle had happened. There was a clink as some large clumsy oaf stalking her, knocked over a glass bottle; she had spun on her heel intending to

MOON

defend herself from the would-be attacker but the air in front of her shimmered and a large reddish glowing cylinder appeared out of nowhere.

What had it said to her?

"Greta...you have been chosen to be my acolyte!"

Not that she had any choice in the matter; the damn thing extended a snake like tube and shoved it over her head. Quick as you like she was in this strangely comforting embryonic sac. Then it got interesting.

Images of the *Guardians* flashed before her eyes, the atrocities they had committed all under the guise of saving mankind. Please! What a joke! *RED* had shown her the real reason they had destroyed nearly all of mankind. In a nutshell,

"Power!"

And then there was the grandfather, their leader. The man who set in motion the actual decimation of so many people! He even sent his son to Earth to help convince the other *Guardians* that they should follow his lead. At least the son - what was his name? *Krys*, that's it - had died before he could complete the misbegotten grandfather's plans. Then there was the grandson, *Chris,* who was still with us, acting all high and mighty. Then

161

bang, that murdering bastard destroyed the first true alien contact that man had ever had without even asking them if they were peaceful all not. No one knows what benefits trade with the *Xhoseti* could have yielded. *RED* was right, the *Guardians* only wanted power and now they had succeeded with that tyrant sitting in his penthouse in City One. Well someone had to take him down a peg or two!

Greta shivered at the prospect of slowly tearing strips of flesh from a captured *Grand Master*.

"Maybe I'll sell his organs to the highest bidder. I'm sure that Jeremy would be interested," Greta let out a high-pitched shriek of delight. Her thick luxurious red hair bounced and quivered as she tossed her head about.

"Now where were we...ah yes, the *ATS* upgrade."

Having shown Greta the atrocities committed by *Krys,* and now *Chris*, *RED* proceeded to enhance her mind powers. Only one true skill would she have though, but that one skill could be used to influence anyone she set her mind on. None would be immune from her charms; from now on anything she wanted she would get others to get for her. Her days of trading were over; no more body part selling; *especially her own!*

162

Then the room went quiet; shadows lurked in the corners, the lamp next to Greta flickered and went dead.

"Oh, you do love to be dramatic Callum! Get your big red ass over here and give me a kiss my love,"

Callum de-cloaked and strode purposely towards Greta, his long graceful strides full of intent.

He always tried to make his presence seem more mystical than it really was, when around her. She loved it and he loved that she loved his performances.

Leaning in close, Callum moved his head close to her neck and breathing in her heady scent. Turning from her neck he placed a deep passionate kiss on her plump red lips. Every time he was in her presence he just wanted to be with her, to do what she wanted. He was like a puppy with its new master, content to do anything just to get a soothing word or a scratch behind the ear.

"Well how did the meeting go with the *Grand Master*?" asked Greta.

"Oh, just the usual boring agenda, except that he wants me to keep an eye on you, hopeful that your message will get lost if we ignore you," replied Callum, sinking into the lounger next to her.

163

MOON

Being this close to her always made his head spin. Her aroma sent his head reeling, a mixture of cinnamon, sherbet and spice; he didn't know if she made him horny or hungry.

"Well Callum, my agents tell me there has been great progress at the module factory. This construction manager seems to be too efficient. It is time we dealt with him; encourage him to not meet the schedule so to speak. If he will not co-operate then have him replaced!"

"Unfortunately, my love, most of the processes have been automated now the basic designs have been completed. To sabotage the mould pours would be to obvious. No, there must be more agent involvement in the assembly of the habitats. Human error so to speak," said Callum thinking out loud.

"I have a few agents willing to take a contract on the Moon. With your influence it should be possible. Callum - you will ensure that they get chosen," Greta paused letting the command sink in.

"Now who else can be of use to me? I know! Jeremy. I may have to entice him a little, you know, rub him up the right way…"

Callum stood up abruptly: red hair burst into fire, his body swelled and shook then erupted into a bright blazing furnace of a fire,

"NEVER!...I WILL KILL HIM FIRST," Callum shouted.

"Sit down my hot-blooded lover. You are the only one for me. Now relax."

Greta reached out her mind to stroke Callum's childish ego but found the way blocked. She had never been blocked before; pushing harder she swept aside his defences and gripping his mind in the palm of her hand and then squeezed.

Callum felt as is his mind was being crushed. The pain was *excruciating*!

Summoning all his will power he tried to fight off this hand that seemed to be crushing his brain. The more he tried to fight it the stronger the grip became and with it the intensity of the pain. Eventually his body and mind could take no more.

Greta watch as Callum struggled against her mind control. He was strong willed, but she was stronger; enhanced with her gift he did not stand a chance. Then, flame doused, he collapsed to the floor, unconscious. Greta threw a pillow at the spot where she imagined his head would make contact with the floor; it landed under his head seconds before it would have made contact. She did not want to explain the bruising to him later.

Now that he was unconscious it would be much easier to manipulate his mind. She set to work placing the psychological triggers that would be activated when required. She placed them in his mind exactly as *RED* had instructed.

*

Chris, standing in docking bay one, surveyed the stacked modules. Every portion of the lunar habitat had to be assembled and checked. The slingshot mechanism on Earth had worked a treat! Now all that needed to be completed were the pre-installation assemblies, checks and subsequent disassembly for *Cata-Portation* to the Moon funnel.

The grey engineers silently got on with the task of assembling the units one at a time. Once assembled and checked, the triple stacked units were decoupled and sent to the catapult. The first of the modules was almost ready to be flung.

Each three-metre diameter R&R module contained four sleep cots. A complement of six sleeper units stacked three high would house the initial complement of workers to start the module assembly process. The first complement of *Worker-Nauts* were already up on the Moon and getting acclimatised in the existing power generation facilities. The eight extra bodies were already making for cramped quarters; official complaints were a daily occurrence. Before any more workers could be sent to the Moon, the R&R modules would need to be assembled and the dome's shaft generators powered up.

*

"Hey Jimbo," shouted Clive over his suit-mic, "watch what you're doing with that plasma cutter, you nearly bust a blood vessel that time!"

Jim leaned harder on the plasma cutter determined to cut through the wall of the module.

"Back off Jim, let the *Cut-Bot* deal with it, you're going to pop a vein."

"Damn, thought that I had it then. Ok bring in the bot."

Standing back, Jim threw his arms in the air and jumped off the top habitation module slowly drifting down to where Clive was waiting.

167

"Control, this is Worker-Naut One, come in."

"This is control, go ahead," came the reply from Teri monitoring the progress.

"We need a cut-bot to open the modules; plasma cutters don't even make a dent in the shell of this new material."

"Stand-by Clive, on the way. Give me a few minutes to load the cutting program and activate the robot."

Twenty minutes later the Cut-Bot entered the dome via the Tunnel-Bot access way and flew up to the top of the three stacked habitation modules.

"Standby WN One, have this tin opened in a few minutes."

There was a clunk as the small cut-bot attached itself to the shell of the module and extended its cutting arm. There was a hiss as the chemical cutter heated up.

"Stand well clear gentlemen. If there's a spill; it will eat through your suits," Teri did not need to elaborate any further. Both men hastily fired their suit's pressure packs, taking them up and onto the access tunnel's bridge.

Viewing the cut-bots progress from the now position of safety, Clive marvelled at how quickly the robot cut through the seemingly impervious material.

Within minutes there was a clunk as the robot broke into the top of the habitation module. Using one of its tubular extremities, the cut-bot excreted a clear gel over the green glowing chemical cutting paste, rendering it inert. The green glow faded rapidly and all that remained of the once incredibly toxic paste was an inert rubbery ring. Scooping up the gel-like ring, the cut-bot deposited the defunct material back in its storage reservoir.

Clive's speaker crackled and came to life,

"Cut complete. Where do you want the off-cut?"

"Dump all off-cuts down at the base of module that they come from; that way we will know where they are. Once we get the assembly hanger completed we can use the off-cuts to make the floor or ceiling or just store them there until we need them. Thanks. Now another cut between module one and two if you please."

"No problem, sending the cut-bot in. Just a moment while it scans the interior."

A laser beam shone out of the bottom of the robot, taking measurements.

169

"All done, moving cut-bot into position."

The robot lowered itself through the aperture, moving past the four sleeping tubes spaced equidistantly around the circumference of the habitation module. Each sleep tube was filled with a clear rejuvenating gel complete with breathing apparatus. Storage lockers lined the space in-between the sleep tubes. Clearly stencilled on the tubes was a number. WN One through Four would occupy the top habitation module. The next two habitation cylinders would house workers five through eight, with the very bottom module containing nine to twelve making up the full complement of the three habitation cylinders.

Settling onto the base of habitation module two, the cut-bot proceeded to chemically burn through the base of the shell. Once cut, the robot went through the same procedure as before and then removed the disk shaped off-cut by-flying out of the habitation modules and placed it at the base of the habitation unit.

"Thanks control, nice work. Now do us a favour and send that cut-bot to the other three habitation modules. We need space for the twenty-four bodies that will be here next week.

MOON

Six hours later the two three storey interlocked sleep habitations were connected to each other and ready to receive occupants,

"Time to head off to the sleep tubes Jim; looking forward to that rest and recuperation we deserve."

*

"Hey Clive, how'd you sleep man?" said Jim shoving a second ball of bacon flavoured recycled paste into his mouth.

After removing themselves from the sleep tubes, both Clive and Jim had made their way back to the old power station for breakfast.

"Actually, surprisingly well. That sleep gel really knocked me out. Kept on having this strange dream though? Not sure if it was real or just a nightmare. Every few hours I think I woke up and saw this strange looking insect like creature running its feelers over my sleep tube. It seemed to be testing it, trying to find a way in," he shuddered, "still gives me the creeps just thinking about it," Clive lifted his arms off the table so Jim could see the raised hairs on the back of them.

"Anyway, just a dream; are you done? This wholesome ball of flavour is getting a bit bland; my body is craving a good fresh bowl of cherries. Time to head back to the dome. The sooner we assemble the mess-hall the better. We must have wasted over an hour just getting here, which means working longer hours to stick to the schedule."

"What was that?" said Luke sitting at the end of the table.

"I thought I overheard you say something about an insect. Sorry for eavesdropping but this may be important."

"Yeah, well mind your own business. Eavesdroppers tend to lose their ears," responded Jim glaring down the table at Luke.

Placing his hand on the second disc, Clive waited for the blue ball to appear then scooped it up and into his mouth.

"Come on Jim, let's go."

*

"Firing bridge harpoon in three...two...one...mark.

Bulls-eye!

Extending bridge core.

MOON

Applying tension."

The construction of the first habitation module was almost complete; only the bridge needed to be constructed, connecting it to the central shaft's platform.

"Attaching Moon-crete applicator to bridge,"

The small triangular shaped construction applicator in place, Clive pushed the large green start button on the face of the machine.

The Moon-crete applicator hummed and clicked, internal mechanisms warming up, heating and mixing the moon dust with the bonding gel in its reservoir.

Within a few minutes, the applicator was inching its way along the bridge's triangular shaped core and a tee shaped walkway started to appear. Once complete, Clive waited a few minutes for the mixture to harden and then walked across the bridge carefully checking his feet for imprints.

"Wow, this stuff sets quickly, one walkway complete! Proceeding to habitation two,"

Following the same procedure as used on Hab-One, soon habitation two was connected to the central generator shaft as well.

173

"Now time for us to crank up the generator,"

Standing on the shaft's platform, Clive stood in front of the southernmost panel marked with large blue letters:

"GENERATOR INITIATOR"

Removing the single bolt with his no-torque driver, the panel swung open easily on its hinges. Inside a large blue button flashed and pulsated.

"Control, I am ready to initiate generator spin. Am I green to go?" asked Clive of Teri who was watching his progress from the control room.

"Hold for initiation worker one. Just running some last minute prestart checks,"

A few minutes later Teri confirmed from the control room:

"All green, I repeat all green, worker one you are good to initiate generator spin. Out."

Pushing the blue pulsating button, Clive stepped backwards expecting to be sucked to the face of the shaft casing. Nothing happened. A few seconds later the generator whirred into life. There was a faint humming noise as the magnetic drives slowly spun up, aided by spurts of expelled pressurised air canisters strategically positioned along the generator's shaft.

The generator shaft started to spin faster and faster creating electricity that could be seen arcing up the internal walls of the shaft.

As the shaft approached maximum rotation the whole building started to shake and vibrate.

"Compensating for artificial gravity, increasing current to stabilisers," came the calm voice over the speaker in Clive's suit.

A few minutes later,

"Maximum generation achieved. You should be feeling the effects of gravity where you are Clive. Report on situation. Over."

"Yes, I can feel the gravity; currently sitting on my ass struggling to get up. Not as heavy as Earth *grav* though, gravity meter shows about point six gees. Standing up, just had the wind knocked out of me! Glad you got that vibration under control though. Thought we were going to see the big man in the stars sooner than expected. So all green here! Out."

MOON

After taking a well-deserved break, Clive and Jim proceeded with the construction process. First the sanitation module with attached *Resyk* unit was lifted into place using the mini *Lift-Bots*. The sanitation modules were placed on the western side of the generator shaft and attached to the shaft platform with a short walkway. Power cables, far too bulky to be transported up to the Moon, had been replaced with microwave transmitters that converted the electricity generated in the shaft for use with a transmitting and receiving unit to power each of the modules.

Over the next few days the mess modules with associated *Resyk* units were attached to the central shaft platform on the eastern side of the dome and now all that remained was to create the assembly hanger. A large, open void had been allocated on the northern side of the building, along with a larger access port, to take the assembled machinery to the central power fabrication dome. Once each of the habitation and assembly domes were complete then construction of the main power fabrication dome would start. By the time the power fabrication models had all been assembled the central dome should be complete.

*

MOON

Travelling along the common ring tunnel that linked the five habitation domes, *Xhespo* wondered at her change in circumstance. Now the humans were stored neatly in these sleeper units just waiting for her to impregnate them with her eggs. No more doubt as to the survival of the *Xhoseti*, only time and opportunity lay ahead. The future seemed secure.

Only one problem though, try as she might her digestive juices could not dissolve the clear cocoons that these humans slept in. There must be another way to get to them while they slept. Confronting them in a group would lead to her exposure and may even end in her destruction. That was not an option; to be discovered before her eggs had hatched would be catastrophic. No, she had to find another way. She had sneaked through the *ATS* access gate to watch and observe these humans, waiting for an opportunity, but so far nothing had presented itself.

Each of the domes she visited was the same. The buildings were identical, the method of erection the same. The way the humans banded together to complete their tasks made it all seem so difficult to single out an individual without raising an alarm. It was almost as if they knew she was there stalking them.

MOON

Then came the day the assembly hanger was completed. She watched as the humans gathered together in the assembly hanger for some sort of presentation.

A man stood on an upturned crate left over from one of the small Moon-crete robots.

"Ladies and ruff-necks, as you all know we are at phase one of the lunar project's completion. Soon we will no longer need to work in these now smelly and disgusting suits for today is the day we use the excess rocket water to create a breathable environment inside the dome," explained Clive, waiting for the cheers coming through his open channel suit speaker to subside.

"I have in my hand a remote that will start the process of generating the atmosphere and turn on the scrubbers so we can get on with life a little more comfortably. Now join me as we count down to a new future for mankind on the Moon,"

"THREE...

TWO

ONE...

MARK."

There was a soft click as Clive pushed the button on the remote. A slight hiss and whirring noise was faintly audible as the oxygen, nitrogen and hydrogen were released into the dome's enclosure.

"Well I expected something a bit more dramatic than that. Still, once the suits come off, it is my pleasure to tell you that some refreshments are available for your enjoyment. Mind you, this is not all just for your pleasure. Each bottle of wine must be sampled and graded so the people back on Earth can use the information in creating products more suitable to the lunar palette. A word of warning, don't drink too much, your bodies will not be used to the alcohol and the gravity. Also, for those of you heading back to Earth tomorrow for a well-deserved break, vomiting inside your transport pod will be most unpleasant. Apart from that, enjoy yourselves and remember to grade the bottles,"

Twenty minutes later, Clive checked his atmospheric meter.

"Right everyone; I will remove my mask first. If I start to turn blue, help me put my mask on as quickly as possible," With that Clive uncoupled his breather unit and with a quick flick of the seal pulled his mask off.

MOON

Taking a deep breath he started to smile, then laugh.

"Now that's what I call fresh air, ha ha. Woooa; feel a head rush coming on, need to sit down for a bit,"

Sitting down on the crate Clive had previously used as a platform to give his speech, he took a few more deep breaths.

"That's better, just needed some time to get used to it. All good now, you can take your masks off. I am sure a bit of wine will give me a reason for this slight headache."

Watching from the corner of the dome, *Xhespo* looked on in fascination as the humans began drinking from the bottles lined up on the table in the room. They would choose one, read the label on it, then put it to their mouth and swallow the contents. Next, each of those that had swallowed the bottle's contents picked up a clipboard with a list of questions and boxes on it. Fascinated with their behaviour, *Xhespo* watched the orderly procedure continue for at least an hour.

"Hey Micky, whatss up man? This wine tastes like swill but man, has it got a kick."

"Hic...yep good stuff this!" replied Micky.

180

"Now we can walk around without that stinking body suit on, I feel like taking it off, know what I mean big boy…Hic."

"Anytime sister! You just say the word and I'm your man. What say you that we head up to the sanitary module for a bit of privacy?"

"Lead on Micky the mouse, haa haa. I'm so funny."

Xhespo watched as the two swaying humans went hand in hand out of the assembly hanger and staggered towards where the humans deposited their waste matter. Following at a slow pace, she crawled along the ceiling watching for an opportunity to pounce.

"Hey baby what you got planned when we get back to Earth, I mean you want to hook up and make babies?" *Xhespo* overheard the male human slurring to the female one.

"Well let's see how tonight goes first. Hic, ha ha."

Looking around furtively, Micky glanced back the way they had come to see if anyone was following them. Seeing no one in sight, he grabbed Shirin by the waist and pulled her close to him.

181

MOON

Xhespo watched as the two humans appeared to be eating each other but neither one screamed in pain as she expected. Then they started stripping off each other's garments.

"Slowly...slowly Micky, ooh I want you so bad. Not out here though, come on let's get a stall,"

Grabbing the male by the hand the female pulled him into the sanitation pod. *Xhespo* followed cautiously. Dropping down from the ceiling above the entrance where the two humans had stood trying to eat each other, she put her mandibles around the corner testing for danger. Just the two humans making heavy breathing noises.

"Ooh Micky you are so smelly...so primitive, it drives me mad with lust."

"Really? You like it?"

"Nah, just shut up and unhook my bra,"

Xhespo turned the corner, watching as the male started tearing at her clothing. Crouching down as low as she could, *Xhespo* slowly crept up on the two humans. The female now had her top off and her chest exposed, large firm breasts now exposed to the elements. One of them the man held in his hand and the other he was trying to eat. The woman had her head thrown back and a small

182

moan of pleasure escaped her mouth. This was really bizarre behaviour to *Xhespo.*

Now within striking distance, *Xhespo* reared up on her four back legs and arcing up her stinger jabbed it into the man's naked back paralysing him immediately. There was a grunt as the man went rigid.

"Micky what the fuck man...don't stop!" it was then that she saw *Xhespo.*

The female stared for a few moments as her blurry vision failed to focus on what had just happened. Reality slowly starting to wind its way from her senses to her brain she opened her mouth to scream. That was when *Xhespo* sprayed her open mouth with sealant gel from her excretion gland just below her mandibles.

The female human fell to the floor no longer holding onto the male and started tearing at the *Xhoseti* gel that now stopped her from emitting any warning calls to her group of possible saviours.

Slowly, circling her prey, *Xhespo* raised her stinger and deposited ten eggs into the hated human who fell paralysed to the floor.

"Musst be quick...musst be quick," hissed *Xhespo* to herself.

183

MOON

Grabbing the unconscious body of the female, *Xhespo* dragged the human out of the room and then secreting more gel, wrapped the body in a cocoon. She then dumped it over the walkway edge. Returning for the other one, she did the same to the male. Once they were both lying at the bottom of the dome, *Xhespo* jumped down as well.

"Hey guys! Hope I'm not interrupting something crude. If I am, put it away and wait until tomorrow," called out Clive.

"I gotta take a piss and even your ugly ass Micky won't stop me from taking it. Guys??"

Peering round the door, Clive was surprised to see no one there.

"Must be in one of the stalls then! Oh well, this cannot wait, I repeat watch out this things goanna blow,"

Grabbing one of the funnels on the wall and pressing it to his loins, Clive proceeded with venting the built-up pressure in his bladder.

"Aaaah! Now that was worth the wait."

Zipping up, Clive turned to walk out of the stall.

MOON

"You kids have fun now! Just don't be late for your shuttle tomorrow."

*

Xhespo dragged the wrapped humans one at a time through the access gate and into the tunnels.

"What to do with them? Leave here and let the hatchlings loose on the other humans or take them back to the mining facility where there is nourishment in the food room?" thought *Xhespo*.

"If the hatchlings are discovered then the humans would send more people to hunt them down. Normally a good thing having prey - think - it is hunter not hunted. *Xhoseti* not strong enough yet! No, hide still best."

Snaring Micky she pulled him along the tunnel until back at the food hall. At the end of the mess-hall was a smaller room where special dietary meals could be prepared if required. This smaller room contained machinery that used the recycled remains from the hall and presented them as realistic looking imitations of the meals requested. The only nutritional difference between these meals and the nutrition balls produced by the table discs was that the requested ingredients that were harmful to the consumer were no longer present.

185

MOON

Dragging the male human into the food preparation room *Xhespo* hung him from the ceiling of the smaller room with more cocoon sap excreted from her gland. Looking at her handiwork, *Xhespo* noticed that the eggs were starting to grow. Small bumps were appearing under the skin of the human and starting to move around as they consumed his layers of fat. Soon they would move on to the muscular tissue before finally consuming the internal organs. The host must be kept alive for as long as possible to ensure healthy hatchlings. This was when the *Xhoseti* were at their most vulnerable.

Taking one more look at her handiwork, *Xhespo* scurried out of the room and returned back to where the cocooned female had been left. Taking hold of the female with her front two arms, she returned to place the hapless human next to her companion.

Xhespo stood back admiring her work; the humans would pay for what they did to the *Xhoseti*.

The time for retribution had begun!

As the hours passed, the hatchlings grew bigger and bigger swelling to the size of a man's forearm.

"Soon my babiess, you will be with me," whispered *Xhespo* with pride.

MOON

A day later both of the humans awoke, eyes bulging, and mouths contorted in silent screams of anguish. The host, now with its internal organs almost completely consumed, went limp, now dead.

"Now come to me my children, come to mommy. It is time to see what delightss this world can give you,"

As one, the miniature *Xhoseti* burst out of their human hosts and crawled out onto the floor. Sensing danger, all twenty hatchlings stood up on their hind legs, tiny claws waggling in the air to fend off this new aggressor.

"It iss me...your queen, do not be afraid. I will teach you and show you the way to hunt our enemy. The humanss!" Xhespo mentally projected to the hatchlings.

"Now bow to me as your leader."

Telepathically bonding with *Xhespo,* the hatchlings gathered round their new deity and made tiny shrieking and hissing noises.

Xhespo, happy with the bonding process signalled for them to be quiet. The brood fell silent. Moving to where the ruptured and torn human corpses hung from the ceiling, she extended one of her front clawed arms and snipped the cords holding them to the ceiling.

187

Moving quickly to the bodies, she excreted digestive juices over one of the human extremities, which, with a hissing sound, dissolved into a nutritious pile of steaming gel. Extending her proboscis, she sucked up the human remains.

Having set an example for her miniature replicants, the horde of mini insectoids ran to the human remains and proceeded to dissolve and digest the human stew.

Soon nothing remained of Micky and Shirin.

Over the following weeks, the *Xhoseti* warriors grew big and strong using the mess-hall's tables. Not as fulfilling as the human remains had been but supplying the nutrient requirements that they needed to grow.

Soon they would be strong enough to hunt in packs. Soon the humans would begin arriving in bigger numbers to complete their power station and then they would feast. The more that arrive the better for her off-spring, as they will absorb any of the technologies that the humans possess. This is the *Xhoseti* gift.

Xhespo still possessed the *Termite* human technologies that had allowed her to construct the great armada of space cruisers used to invade that planet. She had used them to wipe out the human defences

188

surrounding the planet, and land on *Termite* to feast on that weak and pathetic carbon-based life form.

Then, using the alignment of Earth's planets in AD 2492, she had sent the armada through the worm hole only to be destroyed by some kind of super weapon.

How she needed to consume those hated *Guardians* or even better the one they now call the *Grand Master*. Then she could build her ships again and wipe the human race out of existence.

At the moment she had no resources. Her warriors, apart from the freshly grown troops with her, were all dead, destroyed when the worm hole collapsed or eaten by the red fungus. All their experience and knowledge obtained from eating the *Termite* humans lost forever.

Now she must build anew. Train her brood and secure more resources.

The key to destroying the humans is the humans. At least they have gained the knowledge of the two humans the hatchlings consumed. Not much of a beginning but with her expertise, knowledge and experience, gained through ingestion of the hated but soft and tasty human beings, they would thrive and dominate once again.

189

MOON

XHOSETI

"The humanss are doomed!"

*

MOON

EARTH

NUNKI THREE

MOON

Chapter 10

Earth

City Three

Nunki

Down on City Three, or Nunki as the locals preferred to call it, project coordinator Vida stood reviewing her handheld cargo list. Running through the checklist again she scratched her head for the fourth time.

"This is just not right!"

Somehow two worker-naults were missing. It's a straightforward procedure. Board the transport ship, get in the body tube and have a nap. Then wake up in the docking bay down on Earth.

"What was so difficult about that?" Vida bit the top of her pen in frustration. Now she would have to make out a missing persons' report, and in triplicate of all things, just to get a case opened. She bit the pen harder.

"And they probably just missed the transport due to a bloody hangover. These worker types are just so unreliable! *Why don't they just do as they're told!*"

192

MOON

Double checking the roster, Vida stamped her foot on the floor of the docking bay, turned and marched out of the hanger towards her office.

"How many weeks will pass before anyone even took notice of the report? This will ruin any chance I ever had of promotion...Damn it!" she hissed in frustration.

Tears started to well up in her large dark brown eyes.

"I'm going to box their ears when I find out where they are. *That's a promise!"*

Vida wiped her nose on the sleeve of her overall.

Regaining her composure, she sat down at her desk and turned on her screen.

"Well, time to get the more immediate issues resolved. *Bloody workers!* The main power generation dome needs to be completed so I need to get the next bunch of worker-nauts ready," Vida sprayed the air with small specks of phlegm in her agitated state.

Running through the list of candidates on her screen, Vida started crossing out a few names. She could only select twenty-four names with an additional twelve on standby.

193

Only the brightest and best would do, not to mention the healthiest. Life on the Moon would be taxing for even the strongest of candidates, both physically and mentally.

Thinking back to the two missing workers,

"They could have got the space crazies. If that happened there is no telling what they might have done!"

A few cases of space madness had been reported over the past century. Travelling to the Moon, and staying up there for extended periods of time, took its toll on the mental wellbeing of the normally terrestrial bound human physiology. On the odd occasion, panic and paranoia would afflict the apparently stable Luna based occupant. Then, without warning the shakes would start, profuse sweating along with furtive darting of the eyes. Some even started shouting out about seeing demons in every dark corner, even giant insects that hid in the shadows.

"All I know is if the *Grand Master* wants it built, it's going to get built. So, let's get them up there and on with the program. A few brains might get scrambled, but as the saying goes, you can't make an *omelette* without a breaking a few eggs."

Getting back to the task at hand, Vida continued going through the list of possible candidates.

*

Walking through Nunki's trading market, Khanya picked up an apple, raised the green fruit to her noise and inhaled the fresh crisp fruity aroma.

"What do want for this?" she asked the stall owner.

"How about a kiss?" came the cheeky reply from the old bearded man behind the counter.

Leaning in and grabbing the man by the collar, Khanya pulled him close to her. Seeing the bewilderment in his eyes, Willow chuckled to himself, Khanya could be intimidating if she wanted to be.

Planting a big wet kiss on the old man's forehead, Khanya repeated the process until she had completely covered his bald head.

"Stop...stop, please stop that tickles ha...haa."

Khanya released the man, who pulled out a handkerchief and started wiping the top of his head.

The old man looked at Khanya a twinkle in his eye,

195

"Any time you want an apple be my guest, just don't kiss me again... or if you want to..." he let the sentence go unfinished.

"Get out of here you dirty old man."

This time it was Khanya who blushed, turning a darker shade of brown.

Turning from the stall, prize in hand, Khanya turned to Willow who had been trailing her movements.

"We should head up to Greta's apartment," he projected to her.

"Agreed, let's get out of the market and head for the travel shaft. Only cloak when you know no one is watching."

Making their way towards the travel shaft, both Willow and Khanya tried to avoid appearing suspicious. When the next unoccupied transport tube arrived, they both entered and projecting to the minds of those trying to join them that the travel-tube was full. As the tube ascended, both Khanya and Willow cloaked.

Standing in the travel-tube the cloaked pair communicated via mind link only.

"What are you expecting to find out Willow?"

"Not sure, but I have my suspicions that Callum is a bit more intimate with this Greta than he lets on. It may be that his judgement has been clouded by his emotions for her. Maybe we can eavesdrop on their conversation,"

Soon the travel-tube had reached the penthouse habitation level. Stepping out and into the corridor, they silently approached the single red door at the end of the corridor.

A minute later Willow placed his ear to the door hoping to overhear the conversation inside.

"What...what happened? I remember getting mad about you and Jeremy and then nothing. My head is pounding!" Willow overheard a man saying in the room.

"Now, now, my handsome strong man. Come and rest your head over here on my chest. Let Greta stroke your fiery red hair. I'm sure it will pass, just give it a bit of time."

Getting up off the floor Callum went to Greta as instructed and placed his throbbing head on her ample bosom.

197

MOON

Slowly Callum started to feel better. She was right, the pain was subsiding. All he could think about was her scent; the smell of her was intoxicating!

A few minutes passed,

"So, where were we? It is about time we did something about that despot who calls himself the *Grand Master*," continued Greta as if the conversation had not been interrupted.

"What do you mean?" responded Callum.

"Surely you know that he must be removed from that throne of his," said Greta, "and there is only one way to do that. You must kill him."

"What, no wa..."

Callum went silent unable to complete his sentence as Greta reached inside his mind and squeezed again.

"*Stupid man! Do as I say!*"

"Yes my love," came the demure response.

"*When the time is right you will use your powers to kill him. I don't care how you do it or even when, but it must be done and the sooner the better,*" Greta shrieked inside his throbbing head.

MOON

Wincing Callum lowered his head in submission.

"Yes my love, your will is my command," he said out loud.

It was then that Greta's powerful mind picked up the probing interference of Willow standing ear to door just outside her apartment.

"Callum, it would appear that we have some uninvited guests. Bring them to me."

Willow, ear to door had heard enough. Making to turn away and rush towards the transport shaft he tried to move his feet. Something was holding him fixed to the door, he was completely immobilised. Turning his eyes towards Khanya to express his need for help, Willow could just make out the fear on her face as she too stood statue like against the wall.

"Willow, help me! I cannot move," pleaded Khanya.

"Me too!" responded Willow.

Then the door swung open and Willow fell helplessly into the arms of the red headed Callum.

"Willow, what a delightful surprise! I didn't know you would be joining us for lunch. Is this an official visit or just a social call? If I'd have known you where coming I would have made more of an effort," said Callum.

"Oh, I see you have company. Khanya, good to see you as well. Why don't you both come in? What's wrong with them Greta? They are both stiff as a board. Well let's see if we can do something about that,"

Looking at the apple core in Khanya's hand, Callum continued,

"I see you've been eating fruit from the old man in the market. He has been known to put a little sedative in the apples every now and then. Something to do with picking pockets. I must chastise him for that; thought your *Morph-Suits* would have filtered that toxin out though. Anyway, let's get you inside and wait for the effects to wear off then."

Callum carried the small man into the room and placed him on the floor in front of Greta's crouch.

Stepping out into the hallway again, he grabbed Khanya beneath the armpits and dragged her into the room propping her up against the window overlooking Greta's private balcony.

"What shall I do with you?" said Greta to the small man lying at her feet.

"First let me see what you were doing eavesdropping outside my door,"

Greta reached out with her mind and entered Willow's head. As she probed Willow tried to fend off her mind link but to no avail.

"Oh shame, look at the little man... he's crying. Ha...ha. Never mind, it will be over shortly," Greta said, an evil grin spreading across her face.

"There it is, yes...yes! Show me what you heard. My...my, but you were the little sneak. Now what should I do with you. Shall I make you help Callum destroy the despot? No...no, it will be more fun to watch you struggle as you try to tell the *Grand Master* what plans I have for him but cannot. The lock I am placing in your mind will forbid you from telling him about Callum and I."

Mind lock in place, Greta put Willow to sleep then spoke to Khanya.

"You on the other hand need to suffer. I want to see you crawling on your hands and knees begging for me to end your miserable life. Only then will I stop your torment," Greta turned to face the immobile form of the large African woman.

201

Mentally holding Khanya bound as if in chains, Greta hauled the large woman up till she was standing on her tip toes.

"Now stay there until I say you can come down."

Khanya mentally tried to break the mental bonds this red-haired devil of a woman had over her.

"She is too strong, how is she so strong? She does not even have training!" Khanya wondered.

Soon the pain in her thighs and calves became excruciating. As the muscles stiffened and locked into place, lactic acid flooded into the over strained muscles. Tiny striations formed inside the cells causing minute tearing of the fibres. Soon hypotrophy set in and the tears, accelerated by Khanya's *Morph Suit,* started to heal and repair themselves, building muscle upon muscle. At first, small, almost imperceptible bubbles of muscle could be seen rippling along the surface of her legs and calves as the supercharged white blood cells rushed to the damaged area to fulfil their designated task.

Khanya let out a muffled scream of pain as the inflammation levels increased.

More Neutrophils rushed to the damaged cells, releasing cytokines trying to repair the inflamed and

202

damaged cells. Within minutes Khanya's muscles were bulging with the effects of the suits repair process. Each muscle group in her body now screamed in agony as the damaged muscle pulsated and popped when the white blood cells tried to create more fibres to repair the damaged ones. Khanya's muscles were changing shape too rapidly for her suit to adapt to. Cracking...tearing, ripping sounds could be heard as the first of the tendons in her knees tore and broke away from the bone it was attached to, no longer capable of containing the tension caused by the larger and more powerful muscles. Callum stood mutely in the corner; his face held the blank look of a child not recognising or comprehending what it was witnessing.

Greta released the now unconscious Khanya who fell to the floor with a sickening thud, muscles extended and tendons poking out of her joints.

Releasing Khanya from the mind hold, she turned to Callum,

"Now get her fixed. Show her how to use that suit to repair her wounds. I want her ready in a few hours for the next stage of her conversion. I'm going out for a bite to eat. Get that dwarf out of here and back to his own city," barked Greta.

203

"Now move! Don't worry, he cannot tell his friends about us."

Callum picked up the still unconscious Willow and went out and onto the balcony.

Using his mind link with a certain transport cabbie he waited for the floating transporter to arrive.

Ten minutes later his driver arrived in the helium filled vehicle.

"Double your usual fee and no questions. Take my friend to his apartment in City Two," Callum projected the physical address to the mind of the cabbie.

"Sure thing Gov. My lips are sealed. Twice the fee? Well thank you," said the cab driver.

Closing the cab door, the cabbie powered up his hydrogen powered thrusters and sped off leaving a small vapour trail as he went.

Callum watched the cab until he could see it no more then spun on his heel and went back into the apartment, closing the balcony door on the way.

Khanya, no longer held in the mental grip of Greta, was starting to return to her former undistorted shape.

MOON

The *Morph-Suit* was automatically repairing the broken and damaged muscles. Slowly the additional muscles fibres were broken down and removed, using the excess remains to repair the tendons and cartilage that were now reattached to their respective joints and bones.

"Khanya...Khanya, its ok. Wake up! It's me, Callum. You're safe now! You just had a bad fall. Wake up!"

Callum looked over Khanya's body to where the horrific wounds had been only forty minutes ago and was impressed at the effectiveness of the suit to repair the human body. She looked almost fully healed.

"Well, you're going to be stiff tomorrow!" he whispered to himself.

Khanya stirred and groaned, rolled onto her side and vomited.

"Where...where am I. What happened? Can I have some water and ooww. Why do I hurt so much?"

Callum went to the sink and drew a glass of water. He handed the water to her and she gulped down the water in one steady swallowing motion, not slowing for a breath of air.

205

MOON

"Another please," she said handing the glass back to Callum.

"What the hell happened here and why was she so stiff?" she questioned herself mentally. Then she remembered, she and Willow, where was Willow?

Stretching out her mind she probed for his mental signature.

"Nothing...No Willow!"

Then the memories returned.

A look of panic spread across Khanya's face. Hurriedly, she tried to stand up but couldn't move her legs.

"What have they done to me? And where is that devil bitch Greta? Got to get out of here!"

Callum returned with the second glass of water.

Taking the glass from him she sipped the contents slowly, trying to buy more time to come up with a plan and let the suit heal her some more.

"So, are you and Greta an item?" she asked Callum casually.

206

MOON

A broad smile spread across Callum's face.

"I suppose you could say that, but with Greta it's like the weather - one never knows. She's hot and passionate one day, then cold and distant the next," Callum said; a faraway look in his eyes.

"And she will probably take your heart and liver when she leaves. Sell them for a good price as well!" Khanya retorted.

The look on Callum's face could have cut steel.

"Don't you say bad things about her, she's not always nasty to people. You...you just had it coming!"

"She tortured me, and you just stood back and watched. She's a witch! *One of Satan's own!* If I could move, I'd take you to the *Grand Master* and get you expelled from the *Order*."

"Well it's a good job you can't move just yet. Greta will return soon and when she does you will be sorry."

Khanya, using every last ounce of will power, pushed herself up against the wall. Muscles and tendons screaming in protest as she managed to stand upright. Shaky and unsteady, she forced the suit to aid her.

MOON

"Morph blade!"

A laser tipped blade appeared out of the end of her hand, making a crackling noise as the light blazed along its cutting-edge surface.

"Now get out of my way Callum. It is time for me to leave."

"You seriously don't think I can let you go in the state you are in. That would be suicide, not only for me but for Greta too! I think you should join us - that way we three can rule when the tyrant is dead."

"Is that what she's promised you? She will never share power; can't you see that? What has she done to you?"

Khanya made a clumsy lunge at Callum with the blade. The sword hissed as the laser tipped blade sliced through the air.

"Morph shield," said Callum, calmly blocking the clumsy strike with his left arm.

"So that's how it's to be then Khanya."

Morphing his right arm into a large hammer, Callum brought the heavy clumsy weapon arcing downwards onto

208

the unprotected head of his adversary. Khanya collapsed, the top part of her forehead indented from the force of the blow.

The suit had protected her from the majority of the attack; otherwise her entire face would have been a bloody pulp of organic matter.

Watching her lying inert once more on the floor, Callum was impressed to see the leaking wound on her head start to heal, her laser blade gone, absorbed back into the body to be used as a repair resource. Within minutes the almost fatal impression of his hammer blow had disappeared, and smooth shiny new flesh and skin had taken its place.

"Well done Callum," a silky voice whispered in his ear. Greta had returned just in time to watch the pathetic little squabble between her champion and this silly girl. There was no doubt as to the outcome.

"Thank you my love. What shall we do with her?"

"Leave her to me," came the reply, "I know what she needs. So much easier with her mind unprotected!"

Greta entered Khanya's mind to set the blocking locks. Nothing Khanya had seen or experienced could be expressed or communicated to anyone ever again.

209

MOON

Then just for fun Greta squeezed again.

Khany started shaking and moaning on the floor. The occasional muffled scream could be heard escaping her lips as tears ran down her face. Then she was running, her legs powering backward and forwards on the floor, the friction burn marks on her knees from the contact with the floor soon turned bloody and started to pool on the floor.

"Oh, look at the mess your making!" exclaimed Greta, "Stop that at once."

Khanya immediately went stiff. Her wounds started to heal almost immediately as the suit rushed to fix the damaged limbs.

"Now stretch, reach for the sky!" commanded Greta.

Khanya went from a foetal position of protection to a stiff outstretched board on the floor.

"Now up we go,"

As if under the control of some long forgotten demonic power, Khanya rose from a horizontal position on the floor to a straight upright position in a violent arcing motion.

Ten minutes later her already weakened joints started to tear and crack as the muscles bulged and repaired, tearing and remaking the inner fibres. Khanya made no whimper, no scream; no tears ran down her face; luckily for her, she was lost deep down in the darkness of her mind where nothing and nobody could touch her.

Tossing Khanya to the ground like a ragdoll, Greta turned to Callum.

"Well that was fun. See to it that she gets home. Take her yourself and return to your precious *Master*. Tell him that I am reconsidering my ways and that the *Guardians* were right to do as they did. Now go."

The next day Khanya woke in her bed feeling refreshed but hungry and thirsty.

"That was some nightmare, I wonder were Willow is? I must find him."

Khanya stretched and swung her legs over the side of the bed.

"Eish, that hurts. What was I doing last night? I don't remember doing anything strenuous," then the memories of the previous day returned to her.

MOON

"Surely that was just a nightmare? Callum was one of the *Seven*, he was for all intents and purposes her brother," she scratched her dreadlocks.

"I must remember to feed the roots, when was the last time I oiled them?"

Standing up she nearly fell to the floor; legs shaky, she felt nauseous.

"I must find Willow and confirm what really happened. If this Greta has compromised Callum then the Grand Master is in grave danger. He must be warned,"

Khanya hobbled over to her console, turned it on and waited for the machine to warm up. Soon the screen flashed the image of Willow on it and a small round symbol of a letter box appeared below his face. Opening the message, she was surprised to see that the message contained nothing.

Confused Khanya began to type,

"Willow, I had the strangest dream last night. I dreamt that we went to check up on Callum and caught him with Greta. They were conspiring to kill the *Grand Master*. We must warn him," Khanya went to hit the send button, but instead of pushing send her hand started to shake.

212

MOON

Hovering over the delete button, her finger started removing the message without her consent. Message contents removed, Khanya hit the send button, convinced that she had sent the warning to Willow not realising that she too had sent an empty message to him just as Willow had sent to her. It appeared that Greta's mind locks had prevented her from seeing the truth.

*

MOON

XHOSETI

214

MOON

MOON

POWER

PLANT

MOON

Chapter 11

Moon

Main Power Plant Construction

"Right people, time to assemble the Generator Tunnel-Bot," Clive said to the assembled worker-nauts in the hall.

With the aid of the lift-bots, the seven-metre diameter magnet now spilt into quarters were carefully lifted into the assembly room and placed in their allocated positions around a large central shaft. Next the depleted Helium 3 with Ununpentium MC115 reservoirs were attached to the sides of the energy generator shaft. Small tubes linking the central hollow shaft to the reservoirs terminated at the inside diameter of the tube with smoothed-out rounded contours. As the generator rotated, the reservoirs contents would be drawn into the chamber by the pull of gravity as the whole unit spun up. As long as there was product, there would be self perpetuating dosage.

Clive, running his hands over the shiny metal surface of the energy generator shaft let out a whistle,

"Man that looks good! And to think that this gizmo is the answer to man's energy crisis. It looks so simple. Well let's hope it works."

Giving the shaft a push, the tube with attached reservoirs rotated smoothly within the confines of the magnetic field.

"Now that's what I call frictionless motion!

Come in control," said Clive into his microphone.

"Control here. What can we do for you?" came the reply.

"Where is that tunnel-bot? We are ready to insert the generator for transportation to the central dome,"

"On its way worker one. Should be with you in approximately twenty minutes. Suggest you and your crew take a break for awhile. Out."

"Copy that. Out."

Clive turned to his crew who were standing around idle.

"Right people, take a break; go get a cup of something. Be back in thirty. Make sure you eat as well. We've got to make up the time later."

217

MOON

A few grumbles and mutterings filled the room as the crew turned and left.

Soon the assembly hall was empty and it was just Clive alone with his shiny machine.

Twenty minutes later, true to Teri's word, the tunnel-bot arrived.

There was a loud clunk as the tunnel-bot lined itself up with the pre-programmed coordinates for where the access gate would be located.

Minutes later Clive could hear the hissing of the tunnel-bot's lasers cutting into the outside of the dome.

*

Luke loved watching the construction robots build. It was something of an obsession with him. To see man-made equipment perform such complicated tasks in such a coordinated manner filled him with pride. It was as if the machines were synchronised swimmers, all working together for one common purpose but with elegance only obtained by the truly obsessive who lived and breathed their craft.

218

Placed in the centre of the heptagon drawn from the centroids of each of the seven domes, lay a huge construction-bot which had recently been flown in.

Attached to the central construction-bot were seven inert tunnel-bots motionless awaiting instruction.

Luke watched as the main construction machine's lights changed from red to green. Moments later, each of the smaller tunnel-bot's flashing lights turned green as well and began to initiate their programming.

Breaking off from the central construction machine, each tunnel-bot lined itself up with the coordinates for where the domes individual access gates were to be installed. Moving at a leisurely pace, no more than five miles per hour, the tunnel-bots made their way outwards towards the circumference of the soon to be constructed power generation dome. Halfway to the perimeter each tunnel-bot stopped as if awaiting orders.

"This is control," said Teri over the common relay system.

"All domes to acknowledge *Green* for tunnel-bot initiation. In sequence starting with habitation *Dome One* confirm *Green for Go.* Out!"

"Dome One...Green for Go. Out!"

219

MOON

"Dome Two...Green for Go. Out!"

"Dome Three. Hold on control, some teething problems here. Give me a minute," Mario said into his microphone.

"HEY YOU! GET THAT CUTTING TORCH AWAY FROM THE GENERATOR! WHAT THE FUCK DO YOU THINK YOU ARE DOING? HANS...STOP THAT MAN!"

A few tense minutes passed; some loud shouting and cursing could be heard over the open speaker system. There was a thump and more cursing. Then a crack, as the would-be saboteur fell to the ground, blood leaking from the head wound where Hans had hit him with a metal pipe.

"Come in control this is Dome Three,"

"This is control. Go ahead Dome Three,"

"We are Green for Go. Just some spanner monkey that needed an attitude adjustment. Out!"

"Dome Four...Green for Go. Out!"

"Dome Five here, found our rat a few days ago, have her in lockup ready for shipping. Control we are Green for Go. Out!"

220

MOON

"Dome Six...Green for Go. Out!"

"Dome Seven, nothing out of the ordinary to report. All crew eager to finish up and head back home. We are Green for Go. Out!"

"Initiating tunnel-bot burrowing. Out!" said Teri

As one, the tunnelling machines extended their ramps from the rear of the craft and started up their laser cutters. Cutting a smooth laser guided hole in the lunar surface, the tunnel-bots started to descend. Ten minutes later each of the robots had vanished, tunnelling towards their respective domes.

As soon as the tunnel-bots had reached the mapped-out perimeter of the generator dome, the main construction-bot looked as if it lacked purpose.

Standing statue like still, as if at attention, the construction robot appeared to be waiting in anticipation for the command to do its master's bidding.

Hendrik, sitting at his console back in the command and control centre, turned to Teri,

"What do you think, my turn?"

221

MOON

"Yeah I suppose so. I've had all the fun so far. So it's only fair that you take over and claim all the glory you bastard. Ha...ha. Just kidding. The Quality Control Plan has you listed for this one in any case. I couldn't initiate it even if I wanted to. So go ahead, be my guest."

Hendrik typed in the command for the main construction-bot to start the generator dome construction.

A moment later the construction robot opened up its cylindrical body and five gigantic stabilisation arms extended from the central shaft.

At the tip of each arm, were sharp pointed dark rods, very similar to the ones used in the construction of the habitation domes, except proportionally larger. Each one slowly lowered itself onto the Moon's surface and started to vibrate the spike into the lunar surface.

Approximately half an hour later the spikes had reached the hard bedrock that the construction-bot would be anchored to.

"Stopping anchorage process. Verifying bedrock,"

Hendrik pored over the bedrock report on his screen.

"Same as the other bedrock in this area. Looks like we can bed in. Anchorage points are Green for Go. Teri, would you do the honours, I cannot take all the credit you know."

Teri typed in the command to proceed with the anchoring process.

Extending outwards from the anchor arms, large spray nozzles, aided by the low gravity, extended the one hundred metres that would form the perimeter of the generator dome's foundation. The spray nozzle pressure lifts the arms as they stretched further outwards and away from the anchors.

In a similar manner to the method used during the construction of the habitation domes, a thick grey liquid was excreted from the spray nozzles

Once the lunar surface had become saturated from the spraying process, each of the five arms retracted back into the central cylinder.

"Checking phase two.

All Green, starting phase three."

Five gigantic octopus like arms extended outwards from the top of the construction-bots' central shaft towards the generator dome's perimeter. Each of the construction blades hung just above the lunar surface, using the pressurized jet nozzles to hover in place.

The five heavily reinforced arms, now at the domes perimeter, slowly started to rotate around the central shaft, lowering themselves into the thick grey soup as they went.

Upon contact with the ground, there was a shudder as the construction-bot struggled to move the colossal mass of lunar construction material.

"Shit Teri, look at those torque requirements! Back it off, back it off!" screamed Hendrik frantically.

Teri typed in the command to raise the construction arms.

"Right, a little at a time. Shallow cuts are the best way forward here. I might have to use the jets to aid with the heavier passes though," replied Teri.

"Ok. Just keep an eye on the numbers! This will take a lot more manual intervention than anyone planned. Go for it."

Teri cautiously lowered the blades again.

Slowly the arms with their angled blades started to raise the now hardening mass of Moon dust and construction gel upwards, starting the construction process.

Within hours, an outline of the generator dome's structure could be seen rising from the lunar surface. More construction gel and Moon dust were added during the construction phase. Every time the blades shuddered and groaned, Teri compensated for the increased torque requirements with pressurised gas in the spray jets.

Twenty-four hours later the construction-bot lay encased inside the generator dome, becoming the dome's central support shaft as the exterior finished hardening.

"Phase three complete. Time to back off a bit Teri," said Hendrik, "go get something to eat; we need to wait a few hours for the dome to settle and solidify."

An hour later Teri returned, turned on her console and read through the progress report.

"Looks good to me Hendrik. What do you think? Time to initiate the next phase?" questioned Teri hesitantly.

"Let me see. Yep, looks good. Compressive stress at eighty percent of maximum yield; not going to get any

225

harder until the next lunar cycle. Ok, we are *Green for Go* on phase four."

"Initiating phase four." stated Teri.

With the initial three phases of construction complete, the dome's interior volume was filled with pressurised hardening gas. The gas, under pressure, would take the path of least resistance and search out any cracks in the generator domes structure. As soon as the gas came into contact with the cold lunar space it hardened to form an air tight seal. Within the hour, the pressurised dome held steady without any leaks.

"Generator dome sealed," stated Hendrik reading the information on his screen.

"We are *Green for Go* to initiate phase five," he continued.

"Starting phase five," stated Teri, "man Hendrik, damn we're good; next we'll be……. "

"Completing one another's sentences?" Hendrik chimed in.

The residue gas left inside the dome's vast expanse was bombarded with tiny electrical charges, the effect of

226

which forced the gel like coating to stick to the dome's surface like a protective shield.

"Phase five complete," Teri called out.

"Only the access gates to be installed. Then the worker-nauts can get in there and complete the energy generator mechanisms' installations," said Hendrik.

"From the sounds of it, Hab-One has already completed their generator, just waiting on the tunnel-bot to arrive."

"Well they will just have to wait until the rest of the units are ready. The event sequencing does not cater for individual installations."

Within seven minutes, each of the tunnel-bots had reached their programmed coordinates and were preparing to cut into the seven habitation domes to create the air tight access gates.

"That's the last tunnel-bot checked in and lined up," Teri made a clicking noise with her tongue.

"Who knew this would be so easy?"

"It's not done until we fire up the energy generators Teri, you know that."

MOON

"Yeah, but if the progress so far is anything to go by, then we'll all be home in a weeks' time."

Teri rubbed her bloodshot eyes. Squinting at Henrik, "Man, I'm bushed. Let's get the next phase started, then I need some shut eye. Time to put those ice-miners to work."

"You go get some sleep Teri. I'll set the tunnel-bots to shut down when the worker-naut crews start work on the hab-gates locking mechanisms. Now go," said Hendrik.

"Thanks, I'll cover for you when I get back in a few hours."

*

Clive put his breather unit on just in case there was a breach when the tunnel-bot cut through the dome's shell to manufacture the access gate.

Standing to the side of the gate location he watched the gate being laser cut into the structure. He marvelled at how the laser cutter could be tuned to such a fine degree of depth and accuracy.

228

After a few minutes there was a clunk as the dome's access portal came loose and was moved into the assembly chamber still clasped by the tunnel-bot.

The tunnel-bot started to spin the cut-out on a centrally located shaft and using its laser cutters created a slight taper running down the side of the disk.

Clive watched in fascination as the disk received a sticky gel sealant applied over the neatly tapered surface. The disk was intended to be used as the access gate. Once the task was completed, the spinning disk came to a stop.

Next, the tunnel-bot's cutter manoeuvred up to a point just below the apex of the disk and cut four neat, six-inch diameter bolt holes.

Pulling the tapered disk back into the aperture, the tunnel-bot went inert, awaiting instruction.

"Worker-one, this is control come in,"

"Go ahead control,"

"Time for your crew to attach the davit arm and install the gate locks. We await your completion. Out," came the response from Hendrik.

229

MOON

Clive turned around just in time to see his crew enter the assembly hall. Taking off his breather mask,

"Good timing guys.

Open those crates in storage six and get the davit arm installed. All the parts should be there.

Peter, grab the plasma borer and get it aligned to install the cam-bolts.

Andy, you start with the locking mechanism. Remember, follow the installation sequence; crisscross pattern torque system. You only get one shot at this!

Sue, line up with Andy and get those face plates aligned with the strike plates.

The rest of you, assist as necessary.

Now move people, the longer it takes the longer we stay on.

I know that you are all tired but check and double check those alignments. Measure twice, plasma bore once! No mistakes please, this is a once off installation.

You and all who come after you will rely on the security this gate provides. Believe me, if there's a breach in any of the tunnels you'll be glad you did."

230

MOON

Three hours later, locking mechanism in place Andy turned to Clive,

"Right boss, all done. Time to check the seal. I leave the honours to you."

Clive looked at the shiny metal hand wheel resembling a ship's steering wheel. The five tapered shafts that would ram home into the strike plate holes were made of the same shiny metal. Walking up to the circular hand wheel, he took hold of one of the twelve protruding handles and started to turn the wheel clockwise. The exposed offset cam rotated on its shaft and made contact with the first of the five spring loaded locking rods. Turning the wheel further there was a click as the first bolt slotted into place and locked.

"Hmm, nice…very little play," murmured Clive to himself.

Turning the wheel until the next locking bolt pushed into place Clive stood back and pulled out a magnifying scope.

"Get me some engineer's blue Andy,"

Andy went off and returned a few minutes later, can of spray in hand.

Clive took the spray and proceeded to spray the locking bolts until they were completely covered with the blue marking out spray.

Feeling the butterflies fluttering in his stomach Clive continued to spin the lock's hand wheel.

One by one the bolts pressed home and clicked into place.

"Ok. Fit looks good! Now to get on with the pressure test.

Control come in,"

"This is control. Go ahead worker-one."

"We are *Green for Go* on Hab-One assembly hall access door. Out."

Reactivating the tunnel-bot, Hendrik typed in the command to start the seal pressure test. The robot released air into the space between its dome and the gate's surface.

"Hab-One, suggest you don your breather units in case of a leak. If containment is breached, well...I hope

232

you read the fine print in your contracts. Put it this way, the compressed gas will have so much stored energy that you won't feel a thing. Out."

"Thanks control, you're all heart!" replied Clive sarcastically.

After the initial creaking and groaning of the retaining rods when the door was placed under the immense strain of the pressure test, there was a hiss and high-pitched whistle as the air was sucked back into the tunnel-bots tanks.

"Hab-One. Pressure test successful. Good job people. Control Out."

Rotating the gate hand wheel anti-clockwise, Clive slowly unlocked the quality control approved locking system. Taking the inspection scope from his pocket, he started inspecting each locking bolt for any signs of misalignment or minor surface cracks.

"Well Andy, this is better than I had hoped for. At least ninety percent of the bolt surface made contact with the striker plate and apart from a few surface scratches no signs of damage. We are good to go. That's it people, go get yourselves into the sleep pods. We will reconvene in

233

MOON

the mess-hall in eight hours. Yes, you deserve it, a full eight hours.

Thank you all again for your effort."

With those words of praise, the Hab-One crew turned and left the assembly hall, some slapping each other on the back, others high fiving.

*

"This is control Trucker-One. Check in with progress report. Out."

"This is Trucker-One. Nothing to report yet, we are still on route. Will check in when contact with target imminent. Out." came the reply from the ice mining truck.

"Man...those C&C types are control freaks. You would think by now they... steady on Babak or the next boulder you hit will send us into orbit," Sandy cried out, grabbing hold of the arms on her cockpit chair.

The view from the cockpit slowly changed from starry night sky to the sparsely rock populated Moon surface. The truck's retro jets fired again, maintaining line of sight with the landed ice asteroid whilst sending the huge vehicle back down to the Luna surface. Without the jets to change the trucks trajectory, progress would be hindered by the many rocks that littered the Moon's surface, as manoeuvring around or climbing over them took time and resources. This way a more direct path could be taken towards the intended target.

Twenty bumpy minutes later the mining vehicle ground to a halt next to the inert asteroid.

"Wow, the mind boggles at how this huge chunk of rock was landed without making a crater. I read the logs, there were these two astro-miners who brought the rock to the Moon but lost control of it somehow sending it hurtling out of control towards the Moon," said Babak.

Looking up at the asteroid, Sandy noticed the scout ship still attached to its surface.

"Hey Babak, look the scout miner is still attached. Seem to recall that they jumped ship or rock if you prefer at the last moment. Wonder what happened to the crew? No one has heard from them since the incident," said Sandy.

"They could have burnt up all their fuel just getting here and then the rest trying to stabilise this rock," replied Babak.

235

MOON

"Yeah, suppose we'll never know. Without fuel, they would have drifted back to Earth and burnt up on re-entry," said Sandy.

"There was a rumour that some guy witnessed some kind of blue alien entity grabbing the asteroid before it hit the old power station. This must have been where the alien put it. Anyway, enough speculation, we've got a job to do.

Control come in."

"This is control. Go ahead Trucker-One."

"We have acquired target asteroid.

Ready to proceed with anchorage process."

"You are Green for Go on anchorage Trucker-One."

Exiting the cockpit of the mining vehicle, Sandy made her way back to the tether-pod airlock and her mining suit.

Stepping into her suit, she pushed the vacuum seal on the front of her chest and all the air between her skin and the fabric separating her from the insulation gel rushed up past her face.

MOON

Waiting for the panel on her arm to indicate vacuum achieved she went through the sequence list once again.

"Vacuum achieved...Good," the flashing red light next her arm panel turned green.

Reaching up to a clasp around her neck, she turned the locking seal clockwise. There was a sharp click as the seal locked into place.

"Right! Now for the breathing unit,"

She grabbed her round clear faced helmet and placed it over her head hearing the reassuring magnetic lock clamp down. Two canisters ran down the back of her helmet, one used to store the water that was to be used for her atmosphere, the other a scrubber to remove any excess carbon dioxide from her breath.

"Babak, do you read me?"

"Five by five Sandy. Ready to check the helmet seal?"

"Yep...starting fill now.

Nothing's happening.

I repeat there is no atmospheric fill.

237

MOON

Starting helmet check list," stated Sandy slight panic in her voice.

"Sandy, don't panic, just shake your head from side to side for a bit. The kinetic chargers need to be activated so the capacitors can get the required charge to breakdown the water into gas. Jump around a bit if you want."

Sandy shook her head for a second or two. Then there was a pop and the whirl of a tiny fan as the atmosphere flooded into the helmet.

"All green on the air flow. Almost had a heart attack there Babak. Thanks."

Pulling her body into the tether-pod Sandy turned to seal herself in.

"Closing and sealing pod door," she said into her suit microphone.

"Releasing clamps...

Pod is detached...

Firing thrusters."

238

The tether-pod soared up and away from the mining truck, heading toward the closest pillar of ice protruding from the asteroid's surface.

"Looking good Babak. The shaft of ice looks pristine, clean and clear. I'll attach the ground anchor in-line with this shaft.

Heading down to base of asteroid. Out."

Sandy fired the pod's thrusters, heading down to the base of the asteroid.

"Boring anchor hole in asteroid."

Extending the pod's laser cutter, Sandy bore a neat shaft into the base of the exposed asteroid.

"Inserting chem-anchor…now."

Sandy waited until the chemically anchored eye bolt had set, then, using the pod's arm, hooked the polycarbonate tether rope to it.

"Firing deck harpoon."

The tether-pod jerked as the harpoon left the small vehicle; automatic stabilisation thrusters fired to keep it in place.

239

MOON

"Wham bang thank you mam! Damn I'm good. Hit that bedrock first time."

"Lucky Sandy...just lucky. Now get up there and tether the ice. I want to get back to base as soon as possible. I keep having that feeling that something is watching us. Crazy I know but the hairs on the back of my neck keep standing up. Starting to get paranoid and you know what that means..."

"Don't you go getting the space-freaks on me now Babak. I'll be quick as I can. Out."

Flying back up to the shaft of protruding white ice, Sandy bored an anchorage point into the tip of the cylindrical shaped column. Then she inserted a directional, remotely controlled, thruster canister into the hole and moved down the shaft to its base.

"Attaching grapple."

A grappling hook extended out of an opening at the base of the tether-bot. Wrapping itself around the shaft of ice, the grapple winder motor took up the tension. Magnetised collars clamped together, holding the shaft ready for transport should it come free.

"Extending laser cutter...

MOON

Initiating cut."

A few minutes later the shaft of ice came loose. Sandy fired up the thrusters and set the autopilot to control her flight path back down to the mining truck. As the pod turned and headed back to its docking station, the thruster canister fired its pressurised contents, keeping the shaft steady as the tether-pod towed its precious cargo to the storage container on the mining truck.

"Almost with you Trucker-One. Should be hovering above the hydrolysing unit in...one minute."

Babak tracked Sandy and the tether-pod on his view screen.

"Looking good pod-one. I will open the loading bay gate as soon as you give the command."

The tether-pod came to a halt directly above the centre of mining truck. A cylinder, with a spirally sealed gate, extended outwards and up towards where Sandy was hovering.

"Right! Time to load this sucker,"

Taking the pod out of auto-pilot mode, Sandy manoeuvred the pod so the grappling arm had the shaft facing vertically downward.

241

"Starting feed...

Moving shaft towards gate...

Babak, open the spiral, give me three hundred millimetres clearance all round."

Laser beams shot out from the loading gates perimeter locking onto the shaft of ice. Running up and around the full length of the shaft, the laser beams scanned and recorded every millimetre and imperfection of the frozen pillar.

"Scan complete. Looks like three hundred millimetres was pretty close Sandy. Must be those hawk eyes of yours."

"Thanks Babak, now stop it, you're making me blush.

Inserting shaft."

As the icy pillar was pushed into the spiral iris type orifice, the gate's size varied with any change in diameter or imperfections the sensors encountered. As soon as the first seal was breached, the frozen shaft entered a heating chamber which changed the ice into water. Once liquefied, the water entered another chamber where it was pressurised and forced through a filtration screen. In

242

the following chamber the pressurised water was forced through small pipes where it was bombarded with ultraviolet light and then tiny electric currents.

"Ok, looks like you have the package Babak. Should I head off to secure another shaft?"

"Hold on let me check the level gauges,"

Babak tapped his view screen. A few seconds later the water tank readings appeared on his console.

"Looks like we are fifty percent full and sixty percent through processing the shaft. So, no Sandy, this is all we can carry. Get the pod back to the docking station and come join me,"

"Copy that big daddy. On my way. Out."

Sandy typed in the command for the direction thruster canister to detach from the shaft and return to the pod.

Task complete, she headed back to the docking station.

Docking the pod back in its allocated slot, Sandy unbuckled her safety harness and slipped through the access portal.

243

MOON

XHOSETI

It was then that out of the corner of her eye she saw
Xhespo.

*

Xhespo watched the human vehicle approach the
mining station with interest. Here come more resources;
she waggled her mandibles in delight. Looking at her
horde of warriors, she wondered if the time had come to
let them loose on the humans. They were all fully grown
now, having fed on the protein balls provided by the
human feeding tables. Some of them were getting
restless, eager to taste more of the juicy flesh they had
consumed when they were hatchlings.

*"No my faithful children, we must be patient.
Mommy will go and see what the humans are doing here.
Stay inside and out of sight,"* command issued, she
scurried down the corridor and into the mining factory.
There she entered the tunnels dug for the *Xhoseti* by *RED*
and exited onto the Moon's surface.

Being careful not to be seen by the strange pod that
the human female flew up to one of the white shafts
protruding from the big rock, she darted from cover to
cover homing in on her prey.

244

MOON

Soon she had reached the main vehicle and climbed up and onto it. Crouching down low she searched for an opening into the human occupied machine.

After half an hour of testing every hatch and potential access point she could find, her attention was drawn to the flying pod with the female human, as it returned prize in claw.

Squeezing herself as flat as she could, she waited to see if an opportunity would arise when the pod docked, and the human entered the main vehicle.

Waiting and watching the pod slot down into its receiving bay, *Xhespo* could find no means of ingress into the human machine.

Frustration got the better of her and she scampered over to the clear bubble of the cockpit where the human was getting ready to exit the flying pod.

Feeling her way cautiously over the edge of the cockpit, she extended her mandible to try and get some feedback on what the human was doing. Sensing nothing, she raised her head up and placed it against the clear screen hoping to see how the human entered the main vehicle.

245

MOON

For a few eternal seconds, human and *Xhoseti* stared into each other's eyes, one filled with venom and hatred the other startled and scared.

"Damn!...Damn!...Bad!...Bad!...very bad!" shrieked *Xhespo* as she jumped off the human vehicle and back down to the Lunar surface.

Trying to make herself as invisible as possible, *Xhespo* ran as fast as her six legs would carry her back towards the tunnels. Crouching behind the boulders surrounding the tunnel entrance, she cautiously peered over the lowest one to see if the humans had been alerted to her presence.

A beam of light shone from the top of the human vehicle searching for her.

Waiting to see if the humans had alerted any more of their kind...she waited and watched.

After twenty minutes of fruitless searching, the search light on the vehicle went out. Cargo now safely inside, the mining truck powered up and started its return journey to the main energy generation station.

Xhespo clicked her mandibles in anger. That was close...too close.

246

"Musst be more careful...musst be more careful. Patience Xhespo...Patience."

If the Xhoseti are to survive she had to be less invasive.

*

"And I'm telling you I saw some kind of insect peering at me from outside!" exclaimed Sandy.

"Look, I know that you think you saw something, but maybe it's the space crazies. We searched and searched, nothing came up on the scanner. Even the search beam that would have locked onto any heat signature or movement picked up nothing."

"I know what I saw; I'll never forget those eyes. It was the look that a predator gives its prey just before it attacks. I mean the malice in those cold dark eyes. *I was just a piece of meat to it!"*

"Look Sandy, even if you did see something, which I doubt, I mean nothing can survive out there. You need to keep this between us. I cannot afford to lose you. We make such a great team and we have the single source contract to get this chunk of rock mined. I mean, the *Grand Master* recruited us personally."

247

MOON

"Ok! Ok! I'll keep it to myself, but once we get back I'm gone. I don't care if they send me to *Resyk,* I was scared. *I mean really scared!"*

"Fair enough...Now let's head back so we can offload this water for the generator station. They need it to create the domes atmosphere."

A few hours later Trucker-One was within sight of the old power station's control room.

"Control come in."

"This is control. Go ahead Trucker-One."

"Tanks full and ready for delivery. Where do want this bundle of joy? Out."

"Sending pre-planned route to your computer Trucker-One. You are to proceed in-between Hab-Dome Five and Six on the South Eastern side of the plant. Just let the auto-guide take control. Out."

"Roger control. Program is still loading. Wait, steering has been annexed.

Control auto-guide engaged. See you in a few then. Trucker-One Out."

248

The mining vehicle proceeded on auto-pilot towards the generator dome in the centre of the seven habitation and construction buildings.

Coming to a rest at the entrance to the access tunnel ramp, the auto-guide waited for the gate to open before proceeding down the ramp and into the tunnel that would take them to the loading facility.

After passing through the sequence of airlocks, the mining truck proceeded to the main entrance gate. The huge access door swung inwards on the creaking davit arm. The slow but steady progress gave Sandy time to think,

"Did I imagine it? Am I crazy? No, I definitely saw the creature. Will anyone believe me in any case? No probably not. Who was that guy in the mess-hall who said he had seen an insect in the generator hall? Luke, that's his name Luke. Maybe I'll go talk to him."

Sandy shook her head, trying to get rid of the image in her mind. She shivered and let out a little cry at the thought of those eyes again. No, she was out of here, no matter what.

*

MOON

Clive and his crew had just finished assembling the encapsulation-shield machine. The energy-ball boxing machine rested on the floor next to the newly constructed access gate. The tunnel-bot still blocked the gate with its huge tube-like frame.

Curiosity getting the better of Clive, he leaned into the gaping cavity where the newly constructed shield and generator machines would be loaded, when a laser beam suddenly beamed on, scanning his face.

"ALERT...FOREIGN OBJECT DETECTED."

A red light flashed inside the depths of the tunnel-bot. Clive could just make out small snake-like arms slivering around as if to attack any invading entity. He quickly snatched his face back from the loading bay entrance cut by the tunnel-bot.

A bit shaken, he went to stand by the encapsulation machine.

"Come in worker-one."

"This is worker-one."

"We suggest standing well clear of the internal workings of the tunnel-bot Clive. Looks like she has a natural propensity to her privacy. Don't look up her skirt so to speak. Out."

"No kidding control. Standing well clear. Out."

"You are clear to load encapsulation-shield mechanism into the loading bay worker-one."

Held aloft by sonic repulsion, the encapsulation machine slid easily over the assembly room's floor towards the tunnel-bot's loading area.

Already wary of the tunnel-bots internal machinery, Clive stopped well short of the loading area, giving the cargo a soft push. The encapsulation machine continued to slide head long towards the loading bay on the frictionless surface. With no friction to slow its progress the uncontrolled missile was going to smash into the tunnel-bot's shell.

"*Shit!* Now I've done it. All that work just to break it at the last moment!"

Three hundred millimetres from impact with the craft, the tunnel-bot's interior snake like arms shot out of the dark loading bay and grabbed hold of the out of control cargo. Lifting the encapsulation machine effortlessly into the air, the tunnel-bot arms guided it into its cargo hold.

251

"This is control, worker-one. Try to be more careful with the cargo. Even the tunnel-bot has expressed disappointment with your lack of skill. Now proceed with loading the energy generator and be careful. Out!"

Suitably chastised, Clive went back to fetch the energy generator machine. Sliding it along the floor with the aid of the sonic lifters, he brought it to a controlled halt just before the loading bay of the tunnel-bot. As before, arms extended from the dark interior and lifted the machine into the cargo bay.

"Much better worker-one. Even the tunnel-bot is impressed with your motor skills. Now close the access gate once the tunnel-bot has exited your assembly hall. Out."

The tunnel-bot proceeded to close the loading bay and move slowly out of the access door's entrance. Starting up its laser cutters, the tunnel-bot proceeded down the freshly cut tunnel and back to its point of entry. Soon, the tunnel-bot was continuing towards the central power generation dome, to complete the creation of the access doorway from Hab-Dome One's tunnel system.

*

252

MOON

"How we looking Teri?" said Hendrik, looking at her as Teri stared intently at her console.

"All the tunnel-bots have their cargo and have completed the access gates into the generator dome.

Time to start installing the energy pipe-ways."

Each tunnel-bot, now fully embedded into the wall of the energy generator dome, opened their front cargo bay doors.

Excreting Moon dust and construction gel, the tunnel-bots started extruding the piping structures that would house the encapsulation shielding mechanism and the energy-ball generator machines.

"This is going to take a few hours Hendrik. Why don't you take a break? I'll call if something goes wrong."

"Thanks Teri, I need it. I'll keep my personal hailer on. Don't hesitate to use it. See you in a few hours,"

Hendrik left the control room and headed to the mess hall in need of some refreshment.

A few hours later, the pipe bridges constructed, Teri, using the vid-bots, zoomed in on the now completed construction.

253

"Well, nearly there. Just need to load the generators and give them a test run."

Hendrik, looking refreshed, entered the control room.

"Now...now, Teri! A bit of patience please. Let's run through the check list. Someone needs to sign as approved and that someone is me."

Handing him the check list, Teri tapped her foot impatiently.

"Well come on! Let's load the reservoir tanks and do a trial run already!"

"Just a moment. Yes...Yes, it looks good."

Hendrik signed the check sheets.

"Ok, we are *Green for Go* on loading procedure."

Inside the tunnel-bots, the snake like appendages hooked onto the energy generator reservoirs and proceeded to charge the tanks.

"All tanks full and pressurised," said Teri excitedly.

"Starting inertia spin on hab-one generator."

254

MOON

Alternating current surged through the power-ball generator's magnets, causing the shaft to spin.

"Revs are spinning up nicely," stated Teri.

"1000 revolutions per minute.

5000...

12000...

30000...

65000...

90000...

130000 revs per minute.

Wow! This is incredible.

Shaft rotation speed approaching merging speed.

1850000..."

There was a small pop as the contents from the generators tanks melded together.

200000 revs per minute," said Sandy softly, "this is it."

MOON

With a roar, the combined ball of material burst into a bright blue ball of fire and sped out of the generator chamber, down the pipe towards the encapsulation machine.

Running through the continually narrowing pipe, the flaming ball of blue energy dropped into the encapsulation chamber where it was coated in the newly invented *Plasti-Aloid* material.

Slowly, as more and more *Plasti-Aloid* covered the flaming rotating ball of energy, the bright blue light started to fade until no sign of the blue light remained.

With a puff of air, the now dark, inert ball of energy was sent into the generator dome's central shaft.

Travelling along the shaft, the energy ball came to rest in the catapult cup, ready for firing toward the Earth's defence ring catch funnel or down to the planet's cities.

"I'd say that was a positive test run. What do we do with the energy ball?" asked Teri.

"There's a holding bay for the *Aloid* balls, some sort of storage tube in each of the seven catapult feed tubes. I'll program this one to return to hab-one's magazine," replied Hendrik.

256

Energy ball returned and stored in the catapult magazine, Hendrik turned to Teri,

"Right! After that successful test, I suppose it's time to inform the *Grand Master*. Moment of truth, so to speak. Well, this is it! Wish me luck.

Earth Control...Come in.

Earth Control...Come in."

"This is Earth control. Go ahead Moon Control."

"Successful energy-ball creation test.

I repeat, energy-ball creation test is successful!"

"That is good news Hendrik. Congratulations to you and all your crews. We are proud to be a part of this historic moment in mankind's future. I am sure the *Grand Master* will be immensely pleased. Now stand down and await his instruction. I'm sure the council will want to be present at the commissioning ceremony.

Congratulations again.

Earth control out!"

*

MOON

XHOSETI

After the near fiasco with the mining truck, *Xhespo* tried to stick to the tunnels during her exploratory excursions. The only problem was how to enter the newly constructed central dome. She must find a way of ingress without the humans' knowledge. It was then the *RED* came to her aid once again.

Standing on the lunar surface, trying to find a route with enough cover to conceal her approach to the central dome's access port, there was a shimmer in front of her and the glowing red cylinder blinked into sight.

"RED believes that Xhespo requires assistance. What is it that you need?"

"A way into the central dome. The humanss have finisshed the construction of this building and we need to know what iss insside. Something drawss me to it. I know that the Xhoseti can use this new technology to hurt the hated humans," replied *Xhespo*.

"I will build you a tunnel. Follow me," replied *RED*.

With that, *RED* dove down and into the tunnel next to where *Xhespo* was crouching. *Xhespo* followed *RED* at what she presumed was a safe distance.

258

MOON

Reaching the ring tunnel, *Xhespo* watched as the *ATS* paused midway between the tunnel gates of hab-one and hab-seven to start another hillside shaft.

"This tunnel will take you to the central dome where you can make your plans."

Images of the wall entrapped tunnel-bots, with subsequent machinery and piping systems, flashed across *Xhespo's* mind. Of particular interest was the energy-ball encasement chamber. Maybe she could use this to her advantage.

Following *RED*, *Xhespo* watched her ally travel forward making the tunnel, pausing only to add a reinforcement ring every three metres.

Soon they were at the central dome's shell and as before, *RED* created a concealed access gateway.

"Now my Xhoseti warrior, go forth and multiply.

There must be balance."

Xhespo stretched out her mandibles, touching the gateway cautiously. Placing first one, and then the other, on the gate's surface, she probed around softly.

259

MOON

There was a slight feeling of displacement and the next thing she knew, she was standing inside the power-ball generation room.

Heading straight for hab-one's encapsulation chamber she scurried over the mechanism, probing and searching for any clues as to how it worked.

Finding an inspection port, she undid the snap lock seal and crawled inside. Seeing nozzle holes on the inside of the chamber, she wondered what their function was and how they were operated. Climbing out of the chamber, she searched the panel on the side of the machine until she found the words,

"MANUAL OVER RIDE" stencilled in blue letters next to a large red button.

Under the large red button were stencilled,

"HOLD FOR DURATION"

This must be an alternative means of encasing the energy-ball should they require additional coating with the *Plasti-Aloid* material.

"Yess...Yess...This will do the job!" Xhespo whispered to herself.

MOON

"The time to attack the hated humanss iss coming. Soon we will feasst on their ssoft pink flesh. The Xhoseti will rise again!"

Xhespo, plan in mind, scurried out of the energy ball generation hall and out into the new access tunnel.

Heading back along the tunnels, she was actually excited and kept on stopping, lost in her memories of killing and dissolving human limbs. The rest of the warriors will be pleased; they were becoming more and more restless. Each day she struggled to contain their eagerness to attack the humans. Well, now the time has finally come; she only needed the humans to gather together so they can all be dealt with in one coordinated attack.

*

Chris, reading the progress report in his hand, smiled and then smiled again.

"At last it is done. Mankind's energy problems are almost over."

Getting out of his chair, he exited his quarters in the *Guardians'* platform, which now formed part of the planetary defence ring. Striding down the corridor until he came to the communications room, he turned to face the

261

entry door. The door, programmed to recognise his mental footprint, dissolved and allowed him entry.

Inside the communications room, a technician, specially bred in the pods, turned its head to acknowledge *Chris's* presence. The technician's lower torso was melded to the communications panel, which was linked to the *Resyk* centre. The *Resyk* centre provided the body with the required nutrients and a means of disposing of the unutilised remnants of unabsorbed proteins and liquids. This man was always at his station.

Chris addressed the communications technician,

"I would like to send a communiqué to the fabrication plant manager in Guardian."

The technician simply nodded his head, indicating that *Chris* should continue.

"Council, fabrication and construction leads. It is with great pleasure that I can report the completion of the power-ball generator plant on the Moon.

The commissioning ceremony will be taking place in three days' time, at precisely twelve pm City One time, in the central power station dome. You have ample time to make the necessary travel arrangements and will be expected to provide your own lunar environment attire. It

262

will be a twelve hour round trip, so no accommodation will be provided.

A few lunar refreshments will be on hand. Please partake of them sparingly, as the effects on your un-acclimatised bodies may cause a harsh reaction to anything you ingest.

I look forward to your company at this historic event.

Best regards

The Grand Master."

Chris tapped the technician on the shoulder,

"Send that with the highest of priority."

The technician nodded his head and proceeded to type in the message. Soon, the message was being beamed to the quarters of each of the cities' leaders, as well as the fabrication manager in City One.

"Thank you, communications officer one. Now I must check on the progress of the green enforcers. I see no need for the grey engineers either. A time to grow and a time to *Resyk* as the saying goes!"

263

MOON

Whistling as he exited the communications room, *Chris* then headed to the growth pods.

Reaching the growing room, *Chris* enquired as to the progress on his enforcement army.

"The first three hundred are ready to be hatched *Grand Master*. The remaining seven hundred can be kept in the growth pods, ready to be programmed just before being hatched.

They are normally kept at ninety percent of completion, so they are not self-aware until the very last stage of their development," replied the pod technician.

"Good, very good. Time to hatch the three hundred policemen. I hope not to have to use them, but it's better to be prepared for any eventuality.

Plan for the worst and if it does not happen, well then it is a good day.

You may proceed."

"Running genetic program now," stated the growth pod technician.

An hour later, the first of the three hundred giant green enforcers opened their pod hatches and stepped out and onto the growth hall's floor.

Chris, standing in front of the growth pods, could hardly contain his excitement.

"My very own army! Hmm...what to use them for?"

A bit dazed, Enforcer-One...Captain-One, looked at *Chris* expectantly. Then, as one, the three hundred pod grown enforcers got down on one knee.

"*Grand Master*, what is your command?"

The green giant rose from his position and stood to attention, four captain's bars tattooed in white on his bulging forearms.

"Captain...Welcome! I am very pleased to make your acquaintance. Now instruct your men to rise, as they have a lot to do.

First, they will require feeding. Then once sated, you will need to put your troops through some basic training programmes to ensure they are all functioning correctly. If any of your squad shows any sign of defect or disability, you are to report them to me or the pod-technician immediately. Is that clear?"

265

"YES SIR."

The three hundred gigantic green men shouted as one.

"Now call your men to order and follow me."

Chris turned and marched out of the growth pod hall, down the corridor and onwards towards the mess-hall, the three hundred enforcers following their master as instructed.

Entering the mess-hall *Chris* took stock of the grey engineers all resting at the feeding tables. Each engineer had attached the supply tubes to their food pouches and was sitting patiently, waiting for it to fill up. As the enforcers entered, all conversation ceased, and the room went quiet.

"All engineers report to sleep chambers immediately," *Chris* said, barely having to raise his voice.

As one the grey engineers uncoupled their feeding tubes and started shuffling out of the mess-hall intent on doing their master's bidding.

Once the engineers had left the room, *Chris* gave the instruction for the enforcers to feed. Soon the silence was broken with the gurgling noise of the green giants filling up their food pouches.

"Once you have trained and tested your men's capabilities, you will report with them to the catapult transport system. You are to await my command to launch. Each of you will be placed in suspension fluid in the transport cocoons, ready for deployment. Is that clear Captain?"

"YES SIR.

We will be ready Sir. I estimate eight hours to achieve ultimate enforcer preparedness and skills enhancement.

You can count on us Sir."

Chris turned and left the giant green men to the task of filling their food pouches. Hopefully they will only need one feed before the crisis can be dealt with.

"Now to *Resyk* that surplus to requirement troop of engineers."

Walking back down the corridor to the growth pod hall, *Chris* wondered what the most humane way was to get rid of that grey drain on resources.

267

MOON

"They have completed their function! I am surprised that the engineers have not started to disassemble. It was programmed into their DNA after all."

Reaching the sleeping chambers of the grey engineers, *Chris* stepped inside.

Lined up against the walls and ceiling were sleeping pods, all attached to various pipes and tubes. As he watched, a green gas started to fill each of the pods. A few grey arms bashed against the unbreakable poly-carbonate chambers and then all struggling suddenly ceased.

The gas had done its job!

As *Chris* turned to leave the room, a faint hum and sloshing noise could be heard emanating through the pipes attached to sleep pods.

The now dissolved bones and flesh were drained out of the pods and sent back to the *Resyk* centre, to be processed for the next batch of enforcers, so they could utilise it as a resource.

Nothing was wasted!

*

MOON

POWER

PLANT

START-UP

269

MOON

Chapter 12

Moon

Central Power Plant

"Thank you all for coming to this grand opening of the new power plant. As you are all aware, man has a constant thirst that cannot be slaked. For what? Well, energy of course! Even the use of fossil fuels for energy will not suffice," *Chris* paused, watching vice-chairman Jeremy wringing his hands in agitation.

Chris continued, "I, with the benefit of the *Guardian's* knowledge, have ensured that mankind will no longer need to rape the Earth's bounty to slake that terrible thirst. Instead, we can take what we need from the Earth's little brother, the Moon," *Chris* paused again waiting for applause. None came. No one likes a braggart.

The *Seven* were intermingled with the assembled dignitaries and *Chris* had instructed them to motivate those present to clap when it seemed relevant and to issue words of praise at the appropriate moments in his speech. After all, they may not realise it now, but in time they will come to admire the brilliance of his latest creation on the lunar surface.

270

MOON

Each of the *Seven* projected the mental instruction to those in the energy generator hall to clap.

"Thank you, my dear friends and colleagues. I appreciate your support.

Now, there are certain members amongst you who have been less than supportive in the initiation and completion of this magnificent project, but I have found it in my heart to forgive you!"

Jeremy turned to his right and whispered to the political leader at his side,

"Damn man's a peacock! Don't worry, soon we will see if he can turn the other cheek,"

Jeremy raised his hand to his mouth, appearing to stifle a cough, and spoke softly into his com device,

"Now Greta. Initiate project Fire now!"

"As a gesture of good will, I now ask Jeremy, my trusted vice-chairman, to issue the command to start the energy generator plant.

Jeremy over to you,"

Startled, Jeremy coughed again into his hand,

MOON

"Um...Um...Thank you *Grand Master!* We, the people of Earth, are as ever, grateful to you for all you have graced us with. There has never been a more peaceful and harmonious period in mankind's history. Nor I fear, will there be in the future.

As I issue the command to start this gigantic waste of human resources and time, I can only hope that you come to realise that the only way forward for the human race is through the careful use of fossil fuels. *They died so we can live! Now don't let that go to waste!*

GRETA WAS RIGHT!

INITIATE PROJECT FIRE!

NOW START THIS WHITE ELEPHANT!"

"This is control; all hab units initiate sequenced start of power ball generation on my mark.

THREE...

TWO...

ONE...

MARK!"

MOON

There was a rumble and high-pitched whistle as each of the seven power generation units came on line. One by one, they started to spin up to the required two hundred thousand revolutions to fuse the Helium 3 with Ununpentium MC115. Soon, the soft pop of energy ball formation could be heard emanating from the generator tubes. The rumbling noise of the energy balls rushing down the tubes towards the encasement chambers filled the hall, drowning out the chaos that had broken out amongst the assembled delegates.

The worker class and political class leaders were grappling with each other. Old predetermined mind sets and hatreds that had been simmering for centuries came to the boil and violently burst out of control.

Chris, looked on with amusement...let the two guilds get on with releasing their tension. The religious class remained, as always, completely separate from their squabbles.

"What should we do?" came the mind projection from Sven.

"Leave them be, *they will tire of their petty squabbles soon enough. It does detract from the majesty of this great achievement though!"*

273

MOON

The encasement of the last of the bright blue energy balls was nearing completion.

One by one the encased energy balls rattled into the catapult's magazine.

"LADIES AND GENTLEMEN!

YOUR ATTENTION PLEASE."

Chris used his *Morph-Suit* to amplify his voice.

The brawling crowd stopped what they were doing and stared wild eyed at him.

"Watch as the catapult sends those freshly created balls of energy to the defence station's funnel catcher. Soon we will be able to switch off the current power plant and revel in the dawn of a new *energy crisis* free era."

The catapult cup loaded the first of the energy balls and fired. The black encased energy ball sped silently through the lunar atmosphere heading straight for the catchment funnel on the defence ring. From there they would be sent on to the receiving stations just outside each of the terrestrial cities.

*

MOON

Xhespo, drawn by the commotion, stirred from her position up on the ceiling. Drawn to the generator hall by her hatred of the humans, she had watched the humans fight with each other. Surely this was the time to strike. How had they fired the *'catapult'?* This was something she had to learn.

Crawling stealthily down the dome's wall, she entered the tunnel system created for her by the *ATS* entity.

As she returned to the defunct mining plant, a plan had formed in mind.

Instructing eighteen of her warriors to go to the energy-ball hall and await her command, she then selected the two largest to come with her. They would go to this command centre and find out how to fire this *'catapult'*.

*

"This is command, *Grand Master.* First energy ball fired and successfully captured. Shall we fire the remaining energy-balls? Out." Teri's voice boomed over the speaker system in the central dome.

"Proceed. Then place the system on auto. We want production to start as soon as possible. I will give the

275

command to switch over to the new energy receivers on Earth once the first seven balls have been launched towards the planet."

"Acknowledged *Grand Master*. Control out."

Teri proceeded to launch the contents of the catapult's magazine.

Twenty minutes later, all the encapsulated energy balls were on their way to the defence rings funnel catcher.

*

"Right Lynette...I'm off to perform my last walk-down of this old girl. Call it nostalgic sentiment, but I want to be there when the power gets turned off," said Luke to his boss.

"Well don't get too teary on me. You know I'll put it in your file and when evaluation comes around, it's not going to look good if a security guard gets involved with his subject. Sentimentally or otherwise.

Remember it's just a hunk of metal!" replied Lynette.

MOON

Luke put on his breather unit and headed towards the generator room's air lock.

"Right old girl! One last time."

Whistling as he stepped into the air lock and closed the first seal door behind him, he waited for the door lock to change from red to green. There was an audible click as the latch unlocked and the external door swung outwards into the generator hall.

Turning to exit the chamber,

"What the fuck!"

Xhespo, waiting for this very opportunity went straight for Luke's exposed soft abdomen.

Using her stinger, she stabbed him in the stomach, immediately immobilising him. She then proceeded to deposit eggs into his food pouch.

Luke fell to the floor paralysed.

"I knew it, I knew they were real! Oh my god that hurts. Their eating me! No!...No more!. Please...Stop! Stop It! Luke screamed in his mind unable to vocalise his anguish.

"Time to learn, my Xhoseti warriors,"

277

MOON

XHOSETI

Xhespo snatched Luke's left leg in her mandibles and raised it to her mouth. Biting down hard just below the knee joint, the leg soon fell to the floor. Blood gushed out of the gaping wound.

"Now watch my warriors!" she projected to the two *Xhoseti* warriors waiting patiently behind her. *Xhespo* extended her excretion tube below her mandibles and sealed the wound with the sticky gel that she had used to string Shirin and Micky up with. Luke's mutilated leg ceased bleeding almost immediately.

Taking the severed limb and placing it in front of her dribbling warriors, she started to spray the fleshy calve with her digestive juices.

"Join me!" she instructed.

Both warriors needed no invitation as they leaked digestive juices over the severed limb. Soon all that remained of the leg was a pile of steaming human stew. Bones and muscle tissue dissolved into one nutritious puddle. Eagerly the two warriors extended their proboscises to suck up the tasty human.

"After me!" hissed *Xhespo*.

The two warriors immediately stood back awaiting their turn.

278

MOON

Xhespo dipped her proboscis into the pile of steaming gel.

"Aah! Now that hass been a long time coming! Two hundred years have passsed since I have tasted human. Now your turn!

Drink deep my warriors. Learn all you can from this pathetic ssoft human."

Luke stared in horror as these mantis insect like creatures sucked up what remained of his leg and foot. Then his attention returned to his current predicament. No longer intent on feeding on his fat, the baby monsters had turned their attention to the muscle in his other leg.

The pain was excruciating!

Sweat poured from his forehead, wetting his shoulders and torso, his body forced into shock as he was eaten alive.

Then he passed out, saved from the agony of the rest of the consummation process.

Images of Luke's life flashed before *Xhespo's* mind. All her victim's memories were downloaded to her consciousness when she ingested their essence. The only memory she was interested in was one that had been recently acquired.

How to open the sealed door which he had stepped through. Then Luke's memory came to her.

Closing the door behind her, she turned the door's handle until there was an audible clank.

"Now to wait."

A few seconds later the green light on the door turned red. There was a hiss as the room was pressurised. Then the door to the building from where the human had come from opened and swung inwards towards her.

"Leave him.

Now come with me.

There is more knowledge be conssumed and human flesh to drink,"

Xhespo extended her mandibles into the power station's corridor, expecting trouble.

Nothing!

No alarms!

280

No flashing lights!

"Good!

Now, let's go find more humanss."

*

"This is communication officer-one. Come in *Grand Master*. There is an urgent message from city-three."

"Go ahead com-one."

"There is a large crowd gathering at city-one's energy receiving station. Local police are struggling to contain the mass of people gathered there. They appear to be protesting about *Guardian* enslavement and the right of self-rule."

"Thank you, com-one. Tell the catapult master to load the enforcers and keep them on standby. They are only to launch on my command. Destination, city-three power receiver station. If they attack the receiver station the enforcers will put an end to them.

Now send the communiqué to launch the energy balls to each receiver station.

Follow protocol – *Switch*.

MOON

Out!"

With that command received, the communications officer issued the instruction to each of the power receiver station managers to switch off their respective plants and await the arrival of the new energy balls.

"Calling all station managers. This is communication officer one."

"Go ahead com-one," came the reply from the seven power receiver stations of each city.

"Project - *Switch* is active.

I repeat, you are *Green for Go* on project - *Switch*."

One by one each of the power receiver stations powered down, awaiting the arrival of their perspective energy balls.

Almost as one, every man woman and child held their breath as the whirr of machinery wound down, coming to a halt.

Lights went out; city towers were cast into darkness. All around the world families clung to each other; fathers locked their doors, found a weapon of some sort to keep close at hand should it be required.

MOON

Any sound was treated with suspicion.

A baby's cry brought parents rushing to the infant's side, determined to fight off any would-be assailant. Without light, man's primal fear of the unknown reared its ugly head.

The darkness bred fear and fear became the enemy of rational though. In an instant, man was returned to his most basic primitive instincts. The longer the power was down the higher the potential for chaos and anarchy to raise its fiery head.

The human population was on edge.

This was exactly what Greta had been counting on. Gathering her followers, she moved them through the lower streets of city-three and out towards the receiver station.

"Now the time has come to tear down this symbol of those hated Guardians. No more indoctrination, no more strange alien rulers. Tonight, we attack and change man's future forever," Greta thought to herself.

Projecting a mental command to urge her followers onwards, she followed them to the gates of the station.

283

"Now my lovelies...tear those gates down. Throw those oil bombs.

Set this evil establishment a blaze."

As the riot started, Greta shrieked her delight to see the mob under her control to do her bidding.

Soon the receiver plant's outer buildings were on fire.

Operations staff were running out of the building screaming with panic and trying to get away. Most of them were quickly brought to the ground...clubbed until dazed and then doused in oil and set alight. Their screams could be heard all the way back at the habitation towers.

As the buildings burnt, the fire detection system burst its seals and sprayed the fire trying to douse the escalating flames. Without power, the stations fire-fighting systems had no backup energy source to keep the supply pumps running.

The initial explosive jets of water that should have extinguished the fires soon ran out of pressure, becoming a small stream of water then a dribble.

MOON

Power receiver station three burst into flames destroying any hope of project *Switch* fulfilling its objective.

*

"This is the *Grand Master*. Come in com-one."

"Go ahead *Grand Master*," replied the communications officer.

"Send in the enforcers. This wanton act of destruction must be stopped!

Program the rest of the enforcers to maintain the peace at all costs and get them prepped for pod-catapult to the rest of the cities. Now fire those enforcers down to city-three. Out!"

"Yes *Grand Master*."

*

Greta, looking up at the smoke-filled sky, could just make out tiny capsules that appeared to be raining down towards them. It soon became apparent that they were not tiny as they neared her position. Minutes later the cocoon pods impacted the ground and the enforcers were

285

MOON

shot upwards and out of the now cracked transportation pods.

Using her control over her followers she ordered the mob to attack the green giants.

Man and enforcer ran towards each other intent on destruction.

It was then that Greta felt the presence of *RED* in her mind. She had not seen or heard from the *ATS* in many months.

"You are in grave danger Greta. Look up."

As Greta looked up her attention was drawn to a tiny black ball heading for the power receiver station. As it got nearer small cracks in its shell could be seen, allowing bright blue flecks of light to strike out from the speeding sphere of energy.

Realising her mistake, she started to run away from the chaos that had erupted around her. The panic in her mind triggered the release of her control over her followers. Some with raised club or knife stopped what they were doing and stood still, a confused look on their face. The green enforcers appeared confused as well. Programmed to react to violence or civil unrest, they

286

ceased to pummel the tiny humans in front of them now that they had stopped rioting.

"RED help me!" pleaded Greta prostrating herself in front of the glowing red cylinder.

The biomechanical entity paused for a second, then extended its snake like arm and swallowed Greta. She had a last fleeting glimpse at the stunned crowd of both humans and enforcers before the energy ball impacted the destroyed catcher funnel.

A huge mushroom cloud erupted from the epicentre of the explosion, creating a massive wave of destruction as the energy of the blast sped outwards toward city-three.

The wave of energy levelled the entire city, killing all citizens instantly.

Within minutes, no one and no structure remained. The sound of the blast reverberated around the globe and shook any structure higher than ten metres.

Greta grimaced in the embryonic sac of the *ATS*,

"What have I done!...What have I done!"

Time and space seemed as one; then the *ATS* landed on the snowy plains of Antarctica.

287

MOON

Using laser beams, the *ATS* cut a shaft down into the ice. Two miles down the *ATS* stopped, then proceeded to hollow out a small human sized chamber.

After excreting a cocoon like stasis chamber, *RED* woke Greta,

"Time to rest until I call upon you again."

Greta stirred inside the *ATS*,

"As you wish master. I am yours to command."

RED then ejected Greta into the stasis chamber and left, sealing the shaft as it drove to the surface.

"She will be useful in the future. When the Guardians awake, she will awake."

RED then cloaked and flew off towards the Moon to see how *Xhespo* and her warriors were progressing.

THERE MUST BE BALANCE.

*

MOON

Chris, standing in front of the now silent gathering of twenty-one city leaders, started to relay the tragic news of what had just befallen city-three.

"I have some grave news to relay. City-three has been destroyed. Apparently, there was a riot at the receiving station and the catchment funnel was destroyed in the unrest. The green enforcers arrived too late to remove the rioters. I will find out who is behind this hideous crime against humanity.

They are *traitors* to the human race and will pay for their act of destruction. Interrogations will be initiated; no one shall be safe from the thought police. We will find out who they are and who their sympathisers are!

I will start with those present."

Chris started scanning the minds of the men and women present in hall.

Starting his mind scan of the leaders of the now destroyed city-three, it was quickly revealed that the political and religious guide heads were involved in the plot to destroy the receiving station.

"Xhuang, seize the city-three leaders! They will be locked in the mess-hall for now until I am ready to interrogate them further."

289

XHOSETI

The huge Asian man sauntered over to the two leaders, changing his appearance as he walked. Making his bulk larger than one of the green enforcers, he changed the colour of his eyes to that of a blue flaming demon. The two traitors fell to the floor, prostrating themselves before the giant sumo wrestler.

"Please...Please Grand Master! Forgive us. We were not in control of our minds. Greta made us do it. She...She has some sort of mind control ability! We could not disobey her. We will do anything to make up for our mistakes. *We beg you for a second chance!*"

Chris scanned each of their minds, seeing that they were telling the truth,

"Tell me who else is involved. Every following has a hierarchy, now reveal all you know."

Realising that nothing could be gained from holding back any detail the two started to talk.

"We all report to Jer..."

Then the Xhoseti attacked!

The *Xhoseti* warriors had been skulking in the shadows of the energy hall for the past ten minutes, silently awaiting *Xhespo's* orders.

MOON

"Attack my warriors! Attack!" came the mental instruction from her.

As one, the *Xhoseti* rushed down from their hiding place and sprang on the hapless humans.

Stingers ready, the warriors stabbed the exposed human backs without hesitation. In one swift action, eighteen humans lay prone on the floor.

"Seven to me!" screamed the *Grand Master*,

"Willow and Khanya take these traitors and Jeremy to the mess-hall and guard them with your lives. I want them alive!

Now form a semi-circle in front of me. Prepare your shields and weapons.

Give no quarter as none will be given.

These are the Xhoseti warriors I warned you about!"

Byron was the first to react, morphing his arms into laser edged blades; he jumped into the mass of swarming insectiods.

As one, the *Xhoseti* turned their attention to him. Stingers ready, they pounced. Three warriors stabbed

MOON

their lethal paralysing needle pointed extremities into his body.

"SHIELD," Byron shouted.

Instantly the *Xhoseti* stingers were deflected, leaving rippling rings on his suit's protective armour as the thrusts were repelled.

Raising his arms above his head, he brought them down in a downwards arc, slicing the head of the nearest *Xhoseti* warrior clean in two.

Seeing their comrade fall to the ground the *Xhoseti* swarmed over Byron engulfing him in a wave of alien exoskeleton bodies.

Having no means of swinging his blades, Byron changed tactic, replacing his blades with saw toothed spinning wheels.

As he morphed, one of the *Xhoseti,* seeing an opportunity during the split second of the suit's morphing, excreted digestive juices over his changing limbs. The effect was almost instantaneous, Byron's saw bladed arms fell to the floor twitching and spurting blood.

292

He looked at his severed dissolving limbs in horror as the suit immediately sealed up what remained of his gushing extremities.

The *Xhoseti* sensing victory excreted digestive juices all over the shocked human.

Byron's *Morph-Suit* reacted to the corrosive acid attack by projecting a protective cowl over his body, effectively sealing him off from the corrosive environment. Within seconds, the suit started draining Byron of liquids to send oxygen to his lungs, so he could breathe. Within minutes, he felt himself slip into unconsciousness as the suit extracted more and more resources from his body trying to fend off the chemical attack of the *Xhoseti*.

"Passcal help him, help Byron!" shouted *Chris*.

Passcal ran towards the *Xhoseti* engulfed form of Byron,

"Morph laser spear,"

A long shaft appeared in her hand terminating in a laser edged spear head.

Running with the spear pointing horizontally towards the mass of swirling insectoids, she caught the first of the warriors off guard and skewered it through the

293

abdomen. Passcal raised the spear vertical and the insectoid started squirming, trying to remove itself from the weapon impaling it. Seeing that there was no way of removing itself from the spear, it let out a venomous hiss and extended its digestive tube to spray her with its acidic juices.

"*Morph spear...Blades.*"

Two scythe like blades sprang out of the spear shaft's sides and ripped the impaled *Xhoseti* warrior neatly in two. The two halves of the *Xhoseti* tried to stand upright but could not maintain their balance on the three legs that remained. A few seconds passed and then the dissected insect ceased wriggling on the floor and went still.

Seeing their comrade dissected, the *Xhoseti* left the fallen human and turned their attention to Passcal.

Encircling her on both sides in a pincer like movement, the *Xhoseti* closed in.

Spinning her spear shaft around in a sweeping arch, Passcal brought the weapon crashing into the thorax of the first *Xhoseti* within her range. There was a satisfactory cracking sound as the chitin exoskeleton caved in under her blow.

The now wary insectoids circled Passcal watching for any weakness they could exploit.

"Callum with me. We will flank them while they are distracted with Passcal. Sven and Xhuang, you take the left flank. We will attack from the right."

"Morph Shield," said Chris then a shield formed on his left arm.

"Morph plasma blade."

The sword appeared, grafted to his right hand; the searing red hot blade pulsed with energy making a slight humming noise as he swung if in an arc through the air.

Following suite, the demi-god Sven did the same.

Callum, however, morphed his weapon of choice, a huge hammer similar to the one he had used on Khanya. In addition to the hammer, Callum morphed his suit for protection,

"Morph spiked armour."

His skin changed to a dark shade of grey like that of a rhino and sprouted sharp two-inch long tapered spikes.

295

Swinging his hammer experimentally, he grinned, then his hair burst into flames. His eyes shone red like those of a fiery demon freshly spurned from the depths of hell.

Xhuang simply changed the size of his hands!

"Morph gloves."

Xhuang's already massive hands stretched and grew to the size of heavy reinforced car tyres. He smashed them together, causing the air in front of him to shimmer and warp as the shock wave rushed away from him and into the stalking insectiods.

Initially the *Xhoseti* were thrown back by this wave of force but almost instantly jumped back to onto their legs hissing in Xhuang's direction. Seeing that the humans had separated and were approaching them from three sides, the Xhoseti split the remaining fourteen warriors into three packs with the majority remaining focused on Passcal.

Xhoseti and human rushed each other determined to end the others life.

Swarming over Xhuang, the *Xhoseti* warriors excreted their digestive juices, trying to force him to morph into another shape.

Xhuang, aware of the danger to himself should he morph, swatted at the insectiods crawling over his body.

"GET THEM OFF ME!" he shouted, panic clearly evident in his voice.

Sven rushed to his aid, using his shield to batter the stinging, biting warriors on Xhuang's back.

"IT'S NO GOOD! THEY JUST KEEP COMING BACK!"

Raising his plasma sword Sven tried clubbing the insectiods that covered Xhuang's body.

Seeing that his huge hands were having little effect on the nimble *Xhoseti* warriors, he knew he had to change his weapon to one with a sharper edge.

"MORPH CHAINSAW!"

Xhuang's body shimmered as the gigantic hands at the end of his arms shrunk and were absorbed to be replaced with a mechanised tooth covered saw blades. Before he could start the saw blades rotating an *Xhoseti* warrior bit into his right arm at the exact moment he morphed.

His screams of pain only served to intensify the *Xhoseti's* thirst for human blood. As one all fourteen

297

insectoids left their current adversary and rushed towards the screaming human. Digestive juices covered Xhuang's entire body; his morph suit reacted as only it could, encasing him in a protective cowl.

"Need more warriors!" came the mind link command from *Xhespo*.

Three of the *Xhoseti* warriors jumped off the giant human and scurried back to the paralysed bodies lying on the ground. Rearing themselves up and exposing their stingers, each hapless human was injected with *Xhoseti* eggs.

Xhuang's suit was quite literally sucking him dry. Visibly he started to shrink. First, his remaining arm started to shrivel, then the once huge and bountiful belly, that was a sumo wrestlers pride and joy, began dissipating as the stored energy was converted by the suit into the required components to maintain the body cowl. Sensing victory, the *Xhoseti* repeatedly stung at his back and torso.

The initial shock of the *Xhoseti's* latest change in tactics overcome, *Chris* raised his plasma sword high above his head and screamed,

"ATTACK!"

Sven plunged his flaming plasma sword into the mass of writhing insectiods spearing the body of an *Xhoseti* warrior. The blade hissed as it penetrated the exoskeleton of the insectiod and found its way into its softer inner organs. Seeing Sven's success, Passcal threw her spear at the writhing mass covering Xhuang's body, spearing another insectoid. Unfortunately for Xhuang, that was the precise moment that his suit, under immense strain to supply breathable oxygen to his brain, retracted the body cowl that was protecting him from the *Xhoseti* attacks. Passcal's spear found its mark and Xhuang's huge heart. Spear protruding from his chest, Xhuang raised a dissolving arm up to Passcal as if in a plea for help. With the amount of digestive juices covering his body Xhuang melted away in seconds.

Almost instantly, five of the *Xhoseti* warriors extended their proboscises to suck up what remained of the human once known as Xhuang.

"That is disgusting!" exclaimed Passcal,

"All the more reason to destroy these alien creatures don't you think Callum?"

Before Callum could answer, the five *Xhoseti* warriors, now fully recharged, joined their brothers in the attack against the remaining humans.

MOON

"Morph blades," hissed the largest of the five returning *Xhoseti* warriors, who, having recently consumed the remains of Xhuang, meant to try out its newly acquired technology.

Its front mantis like arms started to change shape and take the form of gnarled bony plates with evil looking spiky protrusions. Seeing the newly formed blades protruding from its sockets, the morphed *Xhoseti* warrior attacked Sven striking the bony blades down on his shield. The blades shattered on impact and sheared the mantis arms clean off; leaving round stumps of what was previously a healthy insectiod arm and claw.

Callum, seeing his adversary's weapon break, thrust his plasma blade deep into the *Xhoseti's* neck severing the insectoid's head from its body.

The mortally wounded insectoid flailed about, trying to slash at its adversary with the remaining stumps of it front arms. Passcal morphed another spear and jumping high above the flailing insectoid, drove the spear through it abdomen pinning it to the floor.

"Morph scythes."

The laser sharp blades shot out of the spear's shaft and into the warrior's body, splitting it in two. The severed body of the insectoid tried to get to up onto its legs, fell over and was still.

Shrieking their frustration, the remaining *Xhoseti* warriors encircled Sven, *Chris,* Passcal and Callum.

Standing back to back, the four remaining morphed humans prepared themselves for the *Xhoseti* attack.

As one the *Xhoseti* surged forward stingers pointed towards their intended victims. Callum, tired of the game the *Xhoseti* were playing, jumped high in the air smashing his mighty morph hammer in a downwards strike. The closest two *Xhoseti* were pulverised by his pummelling tactic. The *Xhoseti* lay squashed on the floor, chitin like armour cracked and broken. Digestive juices hissed as it leaked out of the insectoid's glands. The stench of dissolving *Xhoseti* intestines filled the air.

Landing next to the two smashed *Xhoseti*, Callum swung his hammer around in an arc trying to catch the remaining insectoids with the swing. The *Xhoseti* warriors easily ducked or side stepped the clumsy attack.

Recognising the leader of the human party, all nine remaining *Xhoseti* rushed the *Grand Master,* attempting to smother him as they had the other two humans.

301

"*Morph quad arms,*" commanded *Chris*. Four arms with grappling hooks shot out of his torso impaling the nearest four *Xhoseti* warriors. Holding the insectoid warriors with the grappling hooks he sent a mental instruction to Callum and Passcal,

"*Now...Skewer these evil entities,*"

Passcal lowered her spear and ran into the squirming bodies of the two closest to her. Callum swung his mighty hammer swashing the first one in the grip of the *Grand Master* then dispatched the second one in a similar manner.

Re-absorbing his quad arms, *Chris* turned to count the remaining *Xhoseti* warriors. Only five remained, all of whom were intent on destroying him.

Wading into the remaining insectoids, *Chris* swung his plasma sword in a slashing arch, decapitating one of the remaining warriors.

Passcal quickly speared the headless mantis and split its torso in two.

Callum, not wishing to leave the remaining four *Xhoseti* to his master, swung his hammer upwards and down onto the torso of the distracted insectoid, effectively swashing its body as one would a cockroach. The remaining three *Xhoseti* started to back away, then turned to make a run for it when *Chris* morphed a net with rotating spikes and cast it over the retreating *Xhoseti*. The rotating spikes found their mark and sank deep into the *Xhoseti* exoskeletons. Soon the three remaining *Xhoseti* enemies were bundled up ready to be despatched.

Sensing their demise, the three *Xhoseti* excreted digestive juices attempting to melt the human incarceration net. As the net started to melt *Chris* gave the instruction to kill the tied up *Xhoseti* warriors.

Soon the squirming bundle of mantis insectoids were still, and the battle was over.

"Passcal, go and see if there is anything that can be done for the paralysed guild leaders. If not, you will need to destroy the bodies before the *Xhoseti* hatch. Callum, go and help her - we cannot allow them to escape."

Reaching the first of the impregnated delegates, Passcal mentally projected to *Chris*,

"They are all dead! It looks like the Xhoseti are about to hatch. What shall I do?"

"Smash the bodies! Burn them! They must not hatch!" came the reply.

303

XHOSETI

Callum, already aware of the importance of destroying the bodies with the eggs in them, had already started to project pyro-gel over the bodies nearest to him.

"Morph Fire," he projected.

The chemical gel that Callum had ordered his *Morph-Suit* to excrete blazed into life and started to consume the writhing *Xhoseti* filled bodies.

Within minutes, the mini *Xhoseti* were popping out of their human hosts engulfed in flames. Callum watched as the tiny mantis like creatures blazed and crackled. A few even attempted to charge him with their stingers, intent on paralysing their tormentor. He took great pleasure in morphing his shoe into a giant jack boot and stomping on them as one would crush a pesky insect.

Passcal on the other hand was not so efficient. Lacking the ability to create pyro-gel, she morphed her hands into sharp pointed daggers and speared the wriggling *Xhoseti* through the skin and flesh of the now deceased human hosts.

"Got you!" exclaimed Passcal pulling another speared mantis from the guild leader's torso.

Placing the mini insectoid under her boot, she pushed down hard, hearing a satisfying crunch.

304

MOON

She was almost finished with the sixth body when the remaining host bodies seemed to explode and thirty mini *Xhoseti* spewed out and onto the generator hall's floor.

Chris reacted immediately,

"Morph projectile gel!"

Projecting a gelatinous mixture of sticky liquid from his hand he sprayed the mass of hissing *Xhoseti* with it, covering them in this sticky but protein rich liquid.

Initially the mini mantis's struggled and thrashed about trying to remove themselves from the sticky gel. Then, sensing that it could be consumed excreted their digestive juices and began to suck up the human gift.

"What are you doing?" screamed Passcal. *"We want to kill them not feed them!"*

"Wait a while Passcal. All is not as it seems. Soon they will regret swallowing this Trojan gift," replied Chris.

The sticky gel that *Chris* had gifted to the tiny insectoid warriors slowly mixed with the *Xhoseti* digestive juices. As they ingested the protein rich gel a chemical reaction took place, causing the gel to turn into hydrochloric acid. Soon smoke could be seen emanating

305

from the tiny bodies as they melted from the inside. All that remained of the tiny threat was a smoking, oozing pile of gelatine.

The Xhoseti threat was over!

"*Right!* Now to find Jeremy and those traitors. Let's get to the mess-hall. I need to know who is behind this *Xhoseti* attack."

Chris turned and strode meaningfully towards the generators exit.

*

Xhespo and her two trusty warriors continued into the human habitation. The mental images that her warriors had projected to her when they had been terminated by the hated humans only made her more determined to destroy the human race. She must get some of her offspring to Earth.

Coming to a room filled with human equipment, she recognised this room to be the one they called the command and control centre. Mentally commanding her warriors to sneak stealthily into the room and wait for her signal before attacking the two humans sitting at their consoles, the *Xhoseti* waited just behind the hated humans in their chairs.

"This is control. *Grand Master,* come in."

"Go ahead control."

"Our signal from the generator room went fuzzy, are you alright? The signal is back, but I am seeing chaos. There are dead bodies everywhere. What happen? I mean what are those insect like creatures all over the place? Are they dead, please...*tell me they are all dead!*" blurted out Teri, fear making her voice tremble slightly.

"We were attacked by the *Xhoseti,* the aliens that the *Guardians* warned mankind about."

"*You mean they are real!* We always thought that it was just a story to tell our children to stop them misbehaving."

"They're real all right. I think we got them all but be vigilant! There may be more about. Arm yourselves and keep your coms on. We are on our way to you so sit tight. Out!"

Teri turned to Hendrik to ask him what he thought, just in time to see Xhespo stab him in the side with her stinger. Hendrik fell paralysed onto his console, a look of shock on his face.

MOON

Teri screamed and jumped out of her chair making a run for the exit, but the *Xhoseti* warriors were too quick, too nimble for her. She managed to take two steps before being speared in the abdomen. Falling to the ground Teri's terrified eyes locked onto the mantis like insect standing above Hendrik.

Xhespo moved with intent. Taking the male humans forearm in her mouth she bit down hard, severing the limb. As blood spurted out of the still attached portion of the limb, she excreted her sealant gel staunching the wound. Releasing her digestive juices onto the fleshy appendage, she waited. Soon a pile of human drinkable gelatinous mass lay on the floor of the command room. She lowered her proboscis into the steaming fluid and sucked it all up. Waiting for the human's knowledge to flood though her mind, she turned to her two waiting warriors.

"Do the ssame to her but ssave some for me,"

Following Xhespo's example, the warriors each removed one of Teri's forearms and proceeded to dissolve them. When the arm had been dissolved they both extended their proboscises and sucked up what remained of Teri's flesh and bone.

MOON

"Sstand back!" commanded *Xhespo* as she moved to gorge herself on the remaining gel.

A few minutes later,

"So that's how they operate the equipment. Excellent! Now for phase two of the Xhoseti revival!"

Instructing her minions to string the humans from the ceiling and inject them with eggs, *Xhespo* left the room and headed back toward the air lock where her new hatchling warriors awaited her.

Scuttling along the corridor heading back towards the airlock, *Xhespo* paused at the entrance to the mess-hall. Inside there were more humans, one big dark skinned female and a small male. They appeared to be guarding three other humans. As vulnerable as they seemed, now was not the time to get distracted from her main goal.

Reaching the airlock, she turned the doors handle until the red light showed green and it popped open. Inside the hatchlings were busy finishing off the last remnants of the dissolved human male. Seeing their monarch enter the chamber all ten mini instectoids hissed at her presence and reared up on their four rear legs.

309

Waving front mantis arms, they all clambered to get her attention.

"Well my babies, it is time to hide and grow. Follow me."

Xhespo turned and closed the entrance into the human facility. Waiting until the airlock door into the old power generator hall opened, she went through her plan. It all depended on her loyal subjects in the control room. The presence of the humans might cause some problems, but she was sure that her warriors could fulfil their task before the humans realised what is happening.

"Then it would be too late!"

The airlock door clicked and swung open. Crawling through the airlock door she turned to make sure her brood were following. Jumping over the door's sill she marvelled at how quickly they had grown.

Scurrying in-between the silent power generators she headed for the tunnels.

Xhespo scurried along the tunnel until she reached the pipe that would take her and her tiny warriors to the defunct mining station. She knew they must grow and grow quickly; the food hall would be ideal for that task. To be found in this state would end in their destruction at the hands of the hated humans.

Leading them into the silent mining hall and then on to the feeding room, she instructed them to watch. Jumping up and onto the nearest table, *Xhespo* placed her left claw on the dinner plate sized recess. A few seconds later a ball of protein appeared. Extending her proboscis, she sucked up the dark grey ball of protein. Next, she applied pressure to the adjacent disk and with a slight pop, a ball of vitamin rich liquid appeared above it. Sucking up this blue ball of liquid she turned to her see if her attentive students understood what had just occurred.

Each of the mini warriors jumped up onto the table and proceeded to apply pressure to the plates. Soon they were all gorging themselves on this human gift.

Leaving the hatchlings to their feeding, *Xhespo* headed back to the gateway *RED* had provided for her. Placing her mandibles on the gateway she felt the now familiar change in environment and was standing in the tunnel that would lead her to the human habitations. Entering the habitations was not her goal though; she needed to get to the scene of the battle. Her warriors must not have sacrificed their lives for nothing.

MOON

"No, they will be avenged! I will make ssure of it! Ssoon we will all be feassting again."

Travelling along the tunnels that she knew so well, *Xhespo* soon came to the central dome's gateway. After the initial disorientation had dissipated, she cautiously crept to the bodies of the un-burnt humans. Slowly, she put her claws around the dead human's neck and pulled. With a sickening crack and then subsequent squelch, the human head came loose.

She did the same to another six of the human corpses and then rolled the seven heads toward the encasement chamber. Raising her body and exposing her stinger, she pierced the eye of the first human skull depositing a single *Xhoseti* egg into its brain. After depositing her seven eggs into the decapitated human skulls, she undid the clamps on the encasement chamber and placed the first one into it. Closing the lid and clamping it back in place she pushed the large red button marked,

"MANUAL OVER RIDE"

Holding the button down she watched the human head spin inside the chamber as it was encased in *Plasti-Aloid*. Soon the entire human head was gone and only the dark surface of the soon to be loaded, impregnated ball

312

remained. She released the button and with a puff of air the encased head rattled down the piping system to the catapult's magazine ready to be fired.

Soon the catapults magazine had been loaded with *Xhoseti* balls and was ready to be discharged.

"My fine warriorss, the time has come to ssend our future brethren to the human planet. Now rotate the catapult to miss the defence ring's funnel. You have the knowledge from the two humans recently conssumed. Sset the catapult to auto fire once you have programmed in the coordinatess of each of the remaining citiess. The last ball iss to be sent to a place called Mount Kilimanjaro. Ssoon the humanss will regret destroying our sstar sshipss. You must succeed no matter what the cost!

Now do as I command."

*

"Control come in.

This is the *Grand Master*.

Control come in.

Damn it Control, answer me!

313

MOON

The catapult is firing and missing the catchment funnel on the defence ring.

What is going on?" Chris spat angrily into his microphone.

"Khanya, go with Willow to the control room and report to me immediately."

"Yes *Grand Master*. Come on Willow, let's go investigate."

Khanya lead the way down the corridor towards the control room.

As they approached the control room, Willow turned to Khanya,

"I don't know what happened back in the energy generator hall but both Callum and Passcal look exhausted." It was then that *Chris* projected the images of the battle with the *Xhoseti* to their minds

"Be careful. If you encounter any Xhoseti warriors do not let them penetrate your defences with their stingers," projected *Chris* to them both.

"Hell no way am I going to become Xhoseti food!" exclaimed Willow.

"Me neither!" said Khanya seriously.

"Promise me that you will kill me if they get me. Don't let me be a host for them to breed in."

"As long as you promise to do the same for me!" exclaimed Willow.

Approaching the control room, Khanya and Willow both morphed as a precaution.

Willow jumped through the control room's doorway and came face to face with one of the *Xhoseti* warriors. Raising his shiny five bladed hands to be level with his eyes he rushed the creature. The Xhoseti warrior nimbly jumped up and over the small human. Stinger ready, it plunged downward towards the human's head.

"Morph crossbow," shouted Khanya.

Pulling the trigger on the crossbow released a flaming three-sided serrated tipped bolt. The bolt pierced the warrior's thorax and pinned it to the wall.

"Thanks Khanya! I thought that was it."

While the pinned *Xhoseti* warrior squirmed on the wall trying to release itself, the other insectoid made a

315

MOON

rush for the control room's exit. Khanya morphed herself into a large wedge and filled the doorway.

Seeing its means of escape blocked the warrior released its stinger and stabbed at the offending object that blocked its path.

"Hurry Willow! Kill it! I don't know how long my suit will be able to stop its stinger attacks."

The *Xhoseti* warrior, seeing that its attacks were having very little effect released its acid digestive juices all over the human wedge.

"Hurry Willow! Hurry!" screamed Khanya, panic in her voice.

"Morph Axe," screamed Willow.

An axe twice the length of his body appeared at the end of his arms.

Jumping high in the air, Willow swung the giant axe down in an arc. At the last moment the *Xhoseti* warrior sensing it was in danger flung itself sideways narrowly avoiding being split in two. The sudden dart sideways had saved its life but not its legs. Willow let out a grunt of satisfaction as the axe cut through the two left legs of the insectoid that had propelled itself sideways.

316

MOON

The *Xhoseti* warrior toppled over as it lost its balance. Using its front arms and remaining two legs to pull itself upright, it hissed at the small human that had done it so much damage.

Khanya, seeing that the creature was less likely to escape now, changed herself back to her usual humanoid appearance. Pushing her thick dreadlocks out of her eyes,

"Willow stand back! It still has a stinger and that digestive stuff,

Morph crossbow."

The crossbow that she had used to pin the other *Xhoseti* to the wall appeared in her hand. Aiming the spiral serrated bolt at the alien as it stared down Willow, she pulled the trigger. The lethal spiral serrated bolt sped its way to the target, boring a round hole through the *Xhoseti's* thorax and hit the control console behind the creature. The console sparked and crackled then burst into blue electrically ignited flames. Within seconds the console fire had been extinguished as the console sealed itself in hard setting foam, dousing the electrical fire.

The *Xhoseti* stood still, glaring at the hated humans.

317

MOON

"Morph explosive spear," said Willow. A spear the same length as his height appeared in his hand. He flung the explosive tipped spear at the immobile insectoid.

Both Khanya and Willow shouted,

"Shield!" as the body parts of the *Xhoseti* warrior rained down on them.

"Now for the next one,"

Both Khanya and Willow morphed explosive tipped spears and threw them at the *Xhoseti* warrior still pinned to the wall.

After the body parts had fallen to the floor, Khanya turned to Willow and low fived him.

Seeing the bodies of Teri and Hendrik hanging from the ceiling Khanya projected to *Chris* what they must do with them.

"Burn them. They are beyond our help. Burn them now!" came the reply from the *Grand Master.*

Soon the room filled with the burning smell of human flesh.

"Job done...

318

MOON

If it comes to it Willow, do the same for me.

Now let's get back to the *Grand Master*."

*

"Now it's time to see just who or what you are working for," said *Chris,* turning his attention on the first of the city-three leaders.

Scanning the worker class leader's mind, *Chris* began to unravel the web of lies that Greta had spun about the *Guardians*. Without her being present, the bonds she had placed on his mind were soon broken.

"I see that you were under the influence of this terrorist of a woman. And who you reported to...

As I suspected, yes...*Jeremy you traitor!"*

Scanning the other leaders *Chris* soon found out that they all reported to Jeremy, his trusted vice-chairman.

"Sven, bind them.

As traitors to mankind they will be executed as soon as this is over."

"But surely they can be incarcerated *Grand Master*? I mean, we are more civilised than that...This not the

319

twentieth first century," postulated Sven, his head nodding up and down as if trying to get the *Grand Master* to agree with him.

"No, it is the Resyk for them. An example must be made. Now Jeremy, what secrets do you have to tell me?" continued the *Grand Master*.

"Nothing! I did nothing wrong! You are the traitor to mankind...you...you despot!" spat Jeremy, his face contorted with undisguised hatred.

Taking Jeremy's head in his hands *Chris* started to scan the man's mind.

The blocks Greta had placed in his mind were incredibly strong and made stronger with Jeremy's defiance. Soon the effort of keeping the *Grand Master* out of his head made Jeremy start to sweat.

"Aah...There you are...There is the key to unravelling this mystery. My, my, Greta! You have been busy. Now who is your contact? What it's getting clearer...*Callum ...YOU!"*

"Morph sword!" whispered Callum from behind the *Grand Master*.

MOON

Callum struck swiftly, thrusting his newly formed blade into *Chris's* back. The *Grand Master's Morph-Suit* deflected the majority of the piercing attack.

Callum, expecting the suit to repel most of his sword thrust, morphed it again.

"Morph plasma dagger!" a burning plasma blade extended from the tip of the sword and broke through the protective armour of *Chris's* suit piercing his right lung and exited the front of his chest.

"SHIELD!" coughed *Chris* and rolled forward and down onto the floor effectively snapping the blade from its sword base. The dagger now severed from its attachment with Callum returned to its organic form creating a fleshy plug.

"CLOAK!" then the *Grand Master* vanished.

Sven, seeing Callum attack the *Grand Master,* acted on instinct and leapt forward,

"Morph plasma sword!" he screamed raising his flaming sword above his head and bringing it down toward Callum's head.

"Morph spear," said Callum calmly.

321

As the Norwegian deity look alike swung his plasma sword downwards to inflict a mortal wound on his enemy, Callum calmly raised his shield covered arm to ward of the clumsy attack. Sven's plasma blade clanked down on Callum's shield, effectively holding Sven in mid- air for a split second. That was all the time Callum needed to thrust his spear into the torso of his attacker.

"Morph blade," said Callum staring into the blue wide eyes of his victim.

As with the *Grand Master*, the blade pierced the *Morph-Suit's* armour and penetrated into the soft flesh of the human inside the suit. This time Callum's aim was true! The blade went straight through Sven's heart and out of his back. The slowly dying demi-god hung from the end Callum's modified spear.

Passcal sprang into action,

"Morph spear," and charged Callum.

As he had done to Sven, Callum was attacked with Passcal's spear. His suit blocked most of the penetrating attack but Passcal was not finished.

"Morph blade!"

322

Passcal's blade pierced Callum's chest and punched a hole through his rib cage and out of his back.

Seeing his demise in her flaming blue eyes he projected,

"Morph pyro-gel!"

Spraying her with the flammable gel, he then issued the command,

"Morph Fire!"

Passcal burst into flames,

"Morph scythes!" she screeched and fell to the floor rolling in agony.

It was then that Khanya and Willow entered the mess-hall.

Seeing the commotion Khanya ran to her flame engulfed Slavic sister,

"Morph smother," screamed Khanya.

Khanya leap into the air landing on the screaming woman. Her human form morphed to a thick wide smothering blanket. Within seconds the fire had been extinguished and an unconscious but hideously burnt

323

humanoid shape lay under Khanya. Getting to her feet Khanya looked down at the burnt corpse of the once beautiful girl on the floor.

Willow ran over to a rapidly expiring Callum; his torso split were Passcal's blades had torn him apart.

"Morph hammer," said Willow.

Raising his hammer high above his head Willow brought down the heavy weighted hammer on Callum's unprotected skull. There was a crack as his cranium splintered. Willow, now released from the controls that Greta had placed in his mind, brought the blunt instrument down on Callum's head again and again until nothing of the traitors red haired features could be discerned.

"Stop Willow...He's dead.

Now where is the *Grand Master*?" said Khanya softly.

Chris in the corner of the mess-hall de-cloaked. Coughing blood, he projected to Willow and Khanya the events that had just transpired.

"Take these traitors to the *Resyk* room and blend them.

MOON

That is my command!

Now go!" said Chris weakly, red spittle expelled with every word he spoke.

"I need to rest. Get the station up and running again then search for any more *Xhoseti*."

At the edge of the mess-hall the air shimmered and a shiny blue glowing tube appeared. *Chris's ATS* had returned.

Making its way towards *Chris* it stopped in front of him.

"*Entry,*" whispered the *Grand Master*.

A tube extended from the *ATS* and swallowed him. Then the *BLUE* cloaked.

Inside the embryonic sac of the biomechanical entity *Chris* could feel the healing start.

Time and space seemed as one.

Soon the *ATS* had landed in the defence rings docking bay. Still cloaked the *ATS* waited.

MOON

It would take time for the *Grand Master's* wounds to heal.

*

Lynette watched her view screen back in the security room.

"How bizarre!"

The *Grand Master* being attacked by his own warriors? Well she was definitely not going to interfere.

"Let them fight it out. Way above my responsibility grade. *Not going to stick my neck out!"*

She had not risen to head of security by being the first out of the starting blocks. No, instead she preferred to let others do the leading and when they exposed their throats, jump and jump hard on them.

Ten minutes later she turned off her view screen and pulse weapon in hand sauntered into the mess-hall.

"What's going on here?" she said with some bravado.

"Who are you?" challenged Willow.

"Lynette...Head of security here on the old power station."

"Well Lynette, you're just in time to carry out the *Grand Master's* orders.

Take these four traitors to the *Resyk* chamber and blend them.

That is an order!" Khanya commanded.

"Yes Sir.

You can rely on me.

Will you put a good word in with the *Grand Master* for me?"

"Yes! Yes! Just get on with it.

Willow let's search the rest of the facility for more *Xhoseti*. Come on."

With that Lynette frog marched the tied and gagged guild leaders and one now ex vice-chairman to the *Resyk* chamber.

Throwing them into the *Resyk* vat, Lynette waved good bye to the wide eyed and struggling group. She then went to the control panel and after inputting her security

327

clearance codes, set the *Resyk* vat on auto dissolve. Soon all that was left of the traitorous four men was a bloody pulp.

*

Xhespo, still standing in the central generator hall, wondered what she was to do next. She had sent her offspring to the Earth.

"Now what of me? Hide again? The humans will come in force this time."

It was then that *RED* appeared next to her. Extending its snake like appendage the *ATS* swallowed *Xhespo*.

Inside the embryonic sac *Xhespo* noticed that she was not alone. Ten miniature versions of herself lined the walls of the *ATS* embryonic sac. All were in stasis, quiet, immobile, at rest.

Xhespo almost sighed with contentment and then fell into stasis herself.

Time and space seemed as one.

MOON

Soon *RED* was depositing *Xhespo* and her brood in a chamber next to the one for the human; Greta, deep under the Antarctic snow.

Time to Hibernate and Wait!

The Humans Will be Punished!

*** END ***

MOON

XHOSETJ

Acknowledgements:

I would like to thank my father John Stephens for the inspiration of the seven tribes' way back in my youth.

To Jackie Stephens for correcting my grammar; which is always appreciated.

Most of all I wish to thank my wife, Mandy for her patience and encouragement.

*

pentopublish2018

MOON

Printed in Poland
by Amazon Fulfillment
Poland Sp. z o.o., Wrocław